D1531346

# Time Enough

A Carr Collins BOOK

BOOKS BY EMILY KIMBROUGH

Our Hearts Were Young and Gay
*with Cornelia Otis Skinner*
We Followed Our Hearts to Hollywood
How Dear to My Heart
. . . It Gives Me Great Pleasure
The Innocents from Indiana
Through Charley's Door
Forty Plus and Fancy Free
So Near and Yet So Far
Water, Water Everywhere
And a Right Good Crew
Pleasure by the Busload
Forever Old, Forever New
Floating Island
Now and Then
Time Enough

# Emily Kimbrough

# Time
# Enough

## Drawings by Mircea Vasiliu

HARPER & ROW, PUBLISHERS

*New York, Evanston, San Francisco, London*

FIRST EDITION

*Designed by Gwendolyn O. England*

Library of Congress Cataloging in Publication Data
Kimbrough, Emily,   date
   Time enough.
   (A Cass Canfield book)
   I. Title.
PZ3.K5696Ti   [PS3521.I457]   813'.5'2   74-1823
ISBN 0-06-012364-8

To
The full strength of the company
With love

# The Beginning

When Mildred and Sam Jaffe came on board we had been cruising for a week on the Shannon. Their arrival brought the number to ten. Ruth Field came for the last two days and that made the total eleven. This was, as my father used to say, "the full strength of the company."

At Shannon we were a nucleus of eight, the Hacketts, the Stevensons, Sophy Jacobs and I off the same plane, the Garrisons meeting us at the airport. Frances and Albert Hackett had been companions on an earlier trip* but are more widely recognized as major American playwrights. I had introduced them, as we boarded the plane, to the Stevensons, Harvey, architect and painter, and Winifred, always called Biffy, gardener, bird watcher, sailor and an indifferent cook through boredom with the indoors, except for reading. Sophy is known to her traveling companions, on every trip they share, as the General, a generic term for manager, banker, overseer of wines and spirits, photographer, and pivot for the rest of us.

* *Floating Island.*

1

Ellen and Lloyd Garrison reached the airport within a few minutes of our arrival. They had been motoring for ten days in the Irish countryside. Ellen said anxiously she *thought* they'd seen everything in the area they had covered. When Sophy, the Stevensons and I simultaneously and emphatically assured her that certainly they must have seen everything, I thought the Hacketts looked at her questioningly. I knew they were wondering how we could be so positive about a trip we had not shared. We had traveled with Ellen, that was why we could speak with authority. Ellen, covering ground, is not unlike a hunting dog nosing unfamiliar territory. They both explore in widening circles, defining their radii by eccentric dashes to center and back making sure nothing has been overlooked. The reasons for Lloyd's distinction as a lawyer and civil-rights leader include a talent for examining the whole, and each of its parts. Therefore he appreciates and applauds Ellen's ground work.

In extensive correspondence with Mr. Ronald Kearsley, I had been assured two cars would meet us at the Shannon Airport to drive us to Killaloe, less than an hour away. When our bags had all been accounted for and rounded into a mound the size of a haystack, we began a search for these cars and their drivers.

It is, I suppose, because on the several water trips made with friends I had been the instigator and promoter that I am unable to rid myself of a conviction of personal responsibility for every aspect of a voyage—climate, topography and the physical structure of the boat. At the moment the group has cast off from home and the voyage is about to start, I ask myself with bitter self-condemnation why I had had the idea in the first place and then, in a fantasy conceived by panic, could I slip away from the notice of my friends and go anywhere so long as it was far away?

There were no cars outside unclaimed. Every man we saw

2

inside seemed to be on business of his own. We scattered and converged again with the dismal report there seemed to be no one to meet us. The point of one convergence happened to be near the information desk. I was aware of two nice-looking young women standing together not far off. One of them moved toward us.

"Would you then be the party for the *St. Patrick?*" she asked, adding, "Mr. Kearsley told us we were to find you at the information desk."

The cars were fetched. We six plane travelers and our baggage somehow were all packed in. Ellen and Lloyd would follow in the car in which they had been touring; the car and chauffeur would then depart.

Call it, and you will, distressingly juvenile, we will continue to start every trip with, for us, the equivalent of crossed fingers, wishing on a star or whatever ritual others observe. We had come to the country above all others where superstitious safeguards are not mocked.

So the General, by arrangement with the Hacketts and me, leaned out the window of the car she was in, called to the one following:

"Now."

Down the road in Ireland from Shannon to Killaloe, we sang, all passengers and the lady drivers—

"We're off to see the Wizard."

We were on our way!

# 1

No cyclone had brought us to Shannon Airport the 2nd of October. On Sunday, the 7th of May, Sophy had urged me to read in that day's Travel section of *The New York Times* an article by Wilma Dobie about cruising the River Shannon. Halfway through it I had telephoned Sophy the simple message, "Let's go." Her answer was equally terse: "I thought so." And the conversation was finished.

That Sunday was an exasperating and interminable day. Monday was full of promise. Travel bureaus were open, so were libraries and bookshops. Sophy covered the latter. I took to the Irish Travel Bureau and brought home so large a bundle of pamphlets, holding it upright on my lap before me on the bus, I was almost eclipsed. Sophy's loot was skimpier, but mine for all its bulk was unrewarding. Each pamphlet offered a dazzling prospect of beauty of scene and luxury of accommodation, but every boat was operated on the do-it-yourself principle and this was not for us. Our spirits were willing and adventurous but we had to acknowledge to each other, irascibly, the passage of time had weakened our muscles. On other voyages, Sophy had been captain and helmsman; I had been the "decky." That menial's function is to throw around a stanchion or to a lockkeeper the mooring rope, see that the bumpers are hung over the side to avoid scraping against the lock or dock, and retrieve and recoil the mooring rope when the boat is clear again. My aim had not been good, though I had only once hit a lockkeeper full face, but the power behind, however wild the throw, had been respectable. Now fifteen years later, even as I flexed them, I had to admit the muscles wobbled. I recognized too a psychological change and I count this one of the benefits of age. I do not have to prove my stamina. I walk more than a mile every day because I like it. I will never again stand an hour or more at a cocktail party. Therefore, physically and psychologically, I proposed to sit comfortably on a boat while someone else steered and threw ropes, and when all was secured, step ashore to walk my mile or so.

This was not the pattern of "Come Cruising with Book-a-Boat Limited" that promises "a full set of easy to understand maps and charts." The Penguin Group includes, the pamphlet said, "a hirer's hardship-insurance scheme." I did not care to be insured for hardship. The Emerald Star Line "features a flying bridge with alternate steering position." I did not care to assume any steering position, let alone an alternate. Athlone Cruisers Limited promises among its luxuries "a helmsman's seat with side curtains which are absolutely waterproof and have transparent panels." Another luxury is "a stainless steel sink in the galley with pumped hot and cold water, a gas cooker with two rings, grill and an oven." E. Kimbrough will never again be a galley slave, nor occupy a helmsman's seat, with or without side curtains. The luxuries on the Silver Line Cruisers include an echo sounder and compass fitted on the control panel, also a teak steering wheel. Other hands than mine would turn a steering wheel, even one made of teak. The Shannon Cruisers Limited, Mitchell Marine Limited, Cruising Craft Limited, Corma-cruisers, the Flag Line Fleet and the Emerald Star offered conveniences, luxuries, but no people. I telephoned the Irish Tourist Board at 590 Fifth Avenue and the next day wrote a letter to Mr. Sean Carberry, Public Relations Director, Irish Tourist Board.

Dear Mr. Carberry:

At the suggestion of Mr. Hughes with whom I talked on the telephone yesterday I am writing to ask your assistance and advice. In last Sunday's New York Times, May 7th, I read an article about a trip on the River Shannon. The trip sounded so delightful I should like to follow that route with some differences. From the literature gathered at your travel office, I find listed eight-berth cabin cruisers as the largest.

1. Are there larger boats available?
2. Would it be possible to engage a captain?
3. If there are no larger boats available could our trip be planned in such a way that we would tie up near a village or town to make it possible for us to spend each night ashore?
4. Under this plan would it be possible to make reservations ahead to be sure of accomodations at the end of the day?

We should like to do this cruise starting October 2, 1972, for two weeks. . . .

Yours sincerely,

Two days later I had a telephone call from Miss Joan Ennis, who identified herself as a member of the publicity department of the Irish Tourist Board. It was the old Tinker-to-Evers-to-Chance, except that I never heard from Mr.

Hughes or Mr. Carberry again. Miss Ennis said she understood I was interested in a trip on the Shannon. There were some beautiful pamphlets about river cruising. She would mail them to me immediately. I think my emphatic rejection of these startled her; I was remembering the bundle I had carried home. What we wanted, I told her, was a pamphlet about a boat with accommodations for eight to ten people and with equipment that included a captain.

"Oh, a captain?" she echoed dubiously. "Well, that I wouldn't be so sure of. But I'll inquire through our Dublin office."

"Ask them," I urged, "if electric ranges, wall-to-wall carpeting, a helmsman's seat with transparent waterproof curtains can be provided, would it not be possible to find a boat with someone sitting in the helmsman's seat looking through the transparent waterproof curtains?" She sensed an urgency in my voice.

"I'll tell you what I'll do." She spoke more quickly than before. "I'll send a Telex to John Kennedy at our Dublin office."

A line from "The Hunting of the Snark"—"I skip forty years"—is almost an understatement of what the time that followed seemed to Sophy and me. By the phlegmatic calendar it was three months. Sophy, with a concentration at which I marveled, read the books and maps she had culled. I chafed.

On August 29th, out of the Irish mists the shape of a boat emerged by way of a pamphlet entitled *Holidays on the Inland Waterways*. It came with a letter from Miss Ennis. She wrote: "I am enclosing brochure which I received in reply to my Telex. . . . It does not answer my questions. However when you have read through it, please get in touch with me and I will follow up again with John Kennedy at our head office in Dublin." Though dissatisfaction with unanswered questions evidently rankled Miss Ennis's, our bosoms were filled with joy, thanksgiving and relief. The Irish River Floatels Limited—an unfortunate name that made us wince, but no matter—offered one of four "small luxury vessels fully staffed"—those two last, the most beautiful words in any or all the pamphlets I had read—"each to take twelve passengers in single and double berth cabins." Further on, "Each has a staff of four who provide full meals and service on board. All cabins have electric light and wash basins with hot and cold water."

A wash basin in each would be, of course, a very pleasant convenience, but I would have stood in line without complaint so long as, with no assistance from me, a boat would be run, meals would be cooked and beds made. I would have thought there was not a drop more that could be added to this cup of bliss but there was, and far more than a drop, a glorious splash of discovery that the cost of this, including transportation by car from Shannon Airport and return, and excluding only our drinks, would be a modest sum I will not specify lest Floatels and I be held to it. I knew I did not have to wait for words of approval from the friends who had placed such touching confidence in my promise of a cruise on the Shannon. I could hear in my mind only cries of happy astonishment at its cost. I sent the word of accomplishment to them and telephoned to Miss Ennis to hold a floatel from October 2nd to October 16th and ascertain how and when payment should be made. She evidently set the Telexes rolling again, mailing copies to me. A detail in one of them puzzled me: "Could you send brochure setting out measurements of cabins."

Nothing seemed farther from my interest than the dimensions of our sleeping accommodations until I remembered Ellen had asked me to make this inquiry because she had said she wanted to do her morning exercises on the floor there

and wished to be sure there would be space enough. Lloyd, she had added, could do his on the floor in the saloon or on the deck. The dimensions and Ellen's allotment of space were satisfactory.

Now that a man with a name as well as a boat had materialized, I cast off Miss Ennis and her Telexes. Come to think of it, Miss Ennis did the casting off by telephone. She was leaving the next day, she told me, for a holiday in Ireland, hoped we would have a pleasant cruise, glad she had been able to put us in the way of the right people. I wondered if her approaching holiday had been the stimulus for the teeming activity of Telexes during the last two weeks after the drought of silence during the preceding three months.

Mr. Ronald Kearsley, director of Irish River Floatels, made his entrance by letter almost simultaneously with Miss Ennis's exit. He and I engaged in a lively correspondence without benefit of Telex, but with a culmination by way of a telephone and an alarm clock. The alarm woke me at half past four in the morning in Watch Hill, Rhode Island. It was half past nine for Mr. Kearsley in his office at Killaloe, County Clare, Ireland. We settled between us the few remaining details and for me a reassurance. His letters had indicated Mr. Kearsley was a delightful person with the charming manner of a host whose only concern was that his guests have an enjoyable stay. This, he assured me, was his major concern: he would not maintain a rigid schedule (prophetic words). When he knew what things we particularly wanted to see and do, he would make these possible, and would be on the *St. Patrick* himself, though inconspicuously. This was the first time I had heard the name of our floatel and was confident it had a flavor, if not originality, our band would savor.

Since that pleasant telephone conversation had wiped out

the tedium of further details to be checked, I could tear up the list and with Sophy turn my attention to gathering up our flock and deciding such matters as what sort of clothes to take. I asked Mr. Kearsley's advice. His answer was that warm clothes and provisions for rain were essential, although it was quite possible the weather could be warm and sunny, and that indeed was what he hoped.

A friend of mine, staying at a house in Ireland, heard the lady of the manor ask her stableman to remove the halter from a horse grazing in a field that included trees with low, sharp branches, because, she said, the horse might hang himself.

The stableman's answer was:

"He won't! But then he might!"

Mr. Kearsley's advice had the same flavor.

Since there was nothing in it to guide us, we packed according to our own surmises and they turned out to be accurate. We took topcoats, raincoats and sweaters, wool suits and lighter dresses, warm slacks, walking shoes, some rubber-soled sneakers, lighter slippers for evening, and robes or whatever we were accustomed to wear in the evening because we planned to change for dinner. There was not an article of clothing in my luggage I did not wear. No one could say Mr. Kearsley had misled us. We had every kind of weather except snow and were prepared for it. The ratio of sun to rain, fog and mist was the only aspect we had not anticipated. Each of us had spent periods of time in England, long enough to be familiar with that to me most wistful phrase that occurs in almost the daily weather report, "Bright intervals." With characteristically Irish perversity, the intervals on our cruise were fog or rain. The sunny hours by far outnumbered the others.

The reassurance to me the telephone conversation with Mr. Kearsley brought was not, I daresay, reciprocated. Cer-

tainly I never asked him, but in the time between our introduction and our actual arrival I imagined uncomfortably
his almost daily report on a letter from me to his associates
in the office:

"She wrote, you remember, there would be eight passengers
with perhaps one additional. Now she says there will be
eight to start with, two more for the second week and one
added for the last two days. Two of them, Mr. and Mrs.
Stevenson, have to fly home on the 15th, the day before the
cruise ends. Can we fix that up? She says she knows our
cruises start on a Friday, but could theirs start on Monday?
She would like part of the trip to be on the canal. I had
to tell her that's been closed for twenty years. She wrote
that Mr. and Mrs. Hackett would have been in London and
fly from there. Now she says they're coming back to New
York and flying over on the plane with Mr. and Mrs.
Stevenson, Mrs. Jacobs and Miss Kimbrough."

I think he may have added, "What do you make of Mr.
and Mrs. Hackett coming from London to Shannon by way
of New York?"

I asked myself this question, and sometime later I asked
them. I was neither surprised nor enlightened by their explanation of why after a pleasant stay in London they had
returned to New York for ten days and flown from there to
Shannon.

"Why, dawlin'." Frances has one of the loveliest speaking
voices to be heard. It is modulated, cultivated, which means
there is no regional accent except in a word she uses often.
Though her environs are no nearer the deep South than the
outskirts of New York, she says "dawlin'."

"Why, dawlin'," she repeated, not reproachful, but surprised at my lack of understanding, "we came back to New
York and then flew to Shannon because it was much
cheaper." I saw no reason to pursue this.

## 2

Neither the river nor the *St. Patrick* was visible from the parking space in Killaloe where our cars stopped. We were obviously in front of a modest but attractive hotel labeled on a modest signboard THE LAKESIDE, but I had neither the time nor inclination to visit it. At that moment I would have liked to tell my friends to go on ahead, I had forgotten something, and then ask one of the lady drivers to take me back to the airport and from there fly somewhere that would provide asylum and safe hiding. I had got my friends into this. It had been my idea. It would probably be a disaster.

A man came toward us from the far side of the parking lot. I saw that he was tall, his hair dark, worn in a short bang across his forehead, the sides gray, that he was smiling a little diffidently. He did not identify himself, saying only that he and the lady drivers would manage the bags, would we go down, pointing, those steps, we would find the boat immediately below. I did not ask if he was Mr. Kearsley. Perhaps some of his shyness had been communicated to me. I thought, confusedly, Mr. Kearsley was perhaps waiting on

the boat to receive us with a formality due his position. I
went with the others down the steps. It was a long steep
flight, broken halfway by a broad terrace of lawn, garden
beds I could see at the far end, and a wide walk tree-lined.
We were down the second half of this flight of steps before we
saw the *St. Patrick*, a long narrow boat, as barges are and this
was a converted one, and in the opinion of everyone in later
corroboration it was love at first sight. We stepped across a
diminutive gangplank to a small forward deck. I noticed
folding armchairs stacked at one side. From the deck we
moved into an inviting saloon that had on one side a long
couch plentifully supplied with pillows; its length was under
the side windows. What corresponded to a headboard was the
wall between saloon and forward deck. There was a shorter
and narrower couch directly across from the downy one. No
one of us ever sat on it. From the moment we came into the
saloon and simultaneously began unbuttoning and taking off
topcoats, this presented itself as an accommodating place for
them and subsequently for all outdoor accessories. The ac-
cumulation grew to a sizable and disorganized mound, but
the location proved just the right selection, convenient for
matching up whatever was necessary for a quick exit when
some lookout on the deck hailed a sight not to be missed, and
equally convenient for removal on returning.

We did not see immediately the space beyond the saloon
because two young women coming toward us as we entered
blocked our view. They were both attractive but one was a
true Irish beauty, deep blue eyes "rubbed in with a dirty
finger" as her countrymen say, black hair short and curly,
the kind of complexion that typically blooms under the rains
of England and Ireland, dimples visible more often than not
because, we learned, she invariably smiled an acceptance of
any request as if it were the thing she most wanted to do. Her
companion alone would have been noticed as a very attrac-

15

tive girl, with a charming manner and smile. They were introduced by our guide and porter who had welcomed us in the parking lot. Maeve, the beauty, was to be cook, general overseer, and the other girl, Mary, our stewardess. He did not amplify that overseeing would include handling the landing rope. Certainly in specifying a crew rather than a do-it-yourself craft I had thought of a sturdy, muscular seaman. I had not conjured up a sight I shall never forget of Maeve running from the galley as we approached a landing site, usually in the late afternoon. She always wore shoes with very high heels. Reaching the deck, she would seize a coil of rope and with the speed and dexterity of a cowboy in a rodeo toss it either over a stanchion or to a dockkeeper waiting to receive it. If the *St. Patrick* needed to be pulled closer to the dock than our captain could maneuver, she would execute this, pulling the rope and releasing it as required but never once teetering on her high heels. When the mooring was accomplished, she would run back to her galley. Her only preoccupation was with the fresh teacakes she baked each afternoon.

At the moment of our introduction to the two girls and the realization that no one else was there, I expressed a belated recognition that our guide was our host and asked if he were Mr. Kearsley with whom I had had a good deal of correspondence and two telephone calls. I apologized for my sluggishness in identifying him, explaining lamely that the span of the Atlantic Ocean does distort the voice. What I wanted to say was "Why in the world didn't you say who you were up in the parking lot?" but when I saw him blush as he deprecated my apology, I recognized shyness. Our captain, who would be our pilot, Anthony, had not come aboard, Mr. Kearsley told us, but would be ready to take off immediately after lunch. Meantime would we like the girls to show us our cabins? Shyness again, or perhaps some recognition of his position did not permit him to point out the sleeping and other personal facilities.

We followed the girls down a narrow flight of steps, not remotely comparable to the sweeping staircases of an ocean liner, but as someone, I think Frances, said, "Thank God, it's not a ladder." The corridor below that ran the length of the

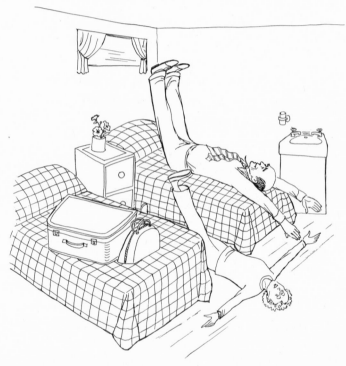

boat was not much wider, nor were the cabins roomy. However, each one included a washstand, a small chest of drawers and a shallow closet. Our girl guides were a little surprised, I think, when Ellen entering the forward double room lay down full length on its floor, at the same time asking Lloyd to stretch out on one of the two beds. My surprise was only momentary because seeing her stretch her arms wide I re-

18

membered her requirements had included space enough for setting-up exercises. When the dimensions of the floor, the firmness of the mattresses were pronounced satisfactory, Ellen said they would not dream of taking that one because it must surely be the best. Simultaneously the Hacketts, who had gone haphazardly into the adjoining room, appeared in the corridor with the declaration they could not possibly occupy the one they had just quit because it was so comfortable. Farther down the corridor beyond the stairway, Biffy stood in a doorway.

"Would you think us piggish if we took this one?" she asked. "It's the nearest to the bathroom and, of course, that makes it the most desirable."

During the clamor of protests and denials that followed this request, Sophy established claim on a single and I found another. To everyone's surprised pleasure there was one cabin that would remain unclaimed. This would provide a storage room for luggage, at the same time making it available so that we need not unpack everything. Though the Stevensons had discovered the whereabouts of the bathroom with tub and the two adjoining "cabinets" containing a john, they were as unskilled as we in the manipulation of the latters' devil's invention. I have cruised on a converted barge in France, another one in England, and also in England a motor cruiser, but I have not yet boarded one that had an adequate "head." The operation is always the same, a pump handle to be wielded with a strong arm and vigorous motion at a rapid pace, but the results vary only from indifferent success to total collapse. The two models on the *St. Patrick* observed faithfully the pattern of their relatives on other waters. One of them responded fitfully to the pump, the other died sometime during the first twenty-four hours of our voyage, though Captain Anthony never admitted its demise.

"Not dead at all," he insisted, "he's just a bit 'coomitose'

from a lazy valve. He only wants rousin' up with the pump."
In our opinion, if he was not dead he had gone into hibernation, and we left him unroused.

When I came upstairs after unpacking—I cannot set down
"topside," I find it embarrassing—I saw for the first time the
far end of the living room—I cannot say "saloon" easily—
was the dining area. Maeve and Mary at our introduction
had formed an involuntary divider. Now I could look beyond to two tables along the windows on either side, each
table set for four. A door at the extremity of this area was
open, letting me recognize the "galley"—kitchen to me.
Maeve was working there.

A long whistle, unmistakably of surprise and pleasure, announced Harvey's arrival at the top of the stairs. He was
carrying a portfoilo and smaller equipment and looking
past me at the tables.

"I didn't see this part before," he told us. "That," indicating, "would be a great work table for me, if you could spare
it. For painting," he added.

With Maeve's enthusiastic approval and help, he set up his
workshop, paper laid on the flat surface of the table, brushes,
paints and tall glasses of water at hand. This was Harvey's
studio and he left it only under persuasion and protest.

At my departure, he was muttering:

"I must get the bridge in this light."

No one else seemed to be aboard. When I asked Maeve,
she said they had all gone off "in bits and pieces." I shook
off an immediate image of some fearful carnage because
Maeve was smiling. "I heard some say," she continued,
"they'd like to see the town, and others of them were going
to look along the shore. They'll be back for lunch. An easy
one thirty, I told them, or whenever it's convenient. Mr.
Kearsley's gone in his car to town. He'll join us later. Anthony's stepped off too, gone for a jar, I've no doubt, but

he said we'd take off about half after two, or somewhat, so he'll be back." I would ask later, I decided, what kind of a jar the captain had gone to fetch.

There was no possibility of catching up with my companions, particularly since they had gone "in bits and pieces," and happily no sense of obligation to be part of a group. I felt instead a glow of satisfaction that at the very outset this trip had assumed the pattern of other trips,* a pattern that sets it apart from all other ways of travel. It is never diagrammed; it is not set down in any brochure. It is simply a happening and it always occurs. No matter how congenial a group, and cogeniality is a prime requisite in assembling a crew, its members invariably scatter at the very moment they go ashore, sometimes individually, sometimes, as Maeve said, "in bits and pieces," but the herd instinct is conspicuously lacking. Reassembled, there is usually as much news to share as if the separation had been of days, not hours.

The path I chose was along the river toward the bridge that spanned it and led to Killaloe proper, but I took a high road, a path at the top of the stairs to the inn that led me through a series of charming gardens and terraces at some height above the river, spreading a happy view of the countryside and the town on the opposite shore, its houses so close together they made me think of women gossiping in the market square, behind and above them the admonitory finger of a church spire. It was not raining but the air was soft and misty. I was too warm in a heavy topcoat and carried it on my arm. From the top of the stairs I saw the others straggling along. Had I not been carrying my own, I probably would not have noticed that every one of our company had removed a top layer.

Already I must have absorbed something of the Irish

* *And a Right Good Crew, Floating Island.*

21

way of seeing things because as I hurried down to join them I realized I was saying to myself, "Now, that's a good omen, surely. We're not going to need all those extra things we've brought for stormy and rainy weather."

The Irish should have been pleased with my quick adaptability to their ways; my prognosis was almost right.

The members of the Explorers Club, self- and spontaneously named, were full of talk and superiority over what they had seen. These were the ones who straggling had trudged some half a mile to the long bridge over the river, crossed it and come into the town proper of Killaloe. They had accidentally converged at the church on the hilltop and read from the guidebook it was supposed to be on the site of Kincora, which in turn was the palace of Brian Boru, the "High" King of Ireland. They had seen the remains of St. MoLua's Oratory beside the church. As a group they had moved on to the Cathedral of St. Flannan, built, they had learned, originally in 782 and on the site of an earlier church. They had admired the heavily carved doorway thought to have been the entrance to the tomb of King Murtagh O'Brian, who died in 1120, and a beautiful twelfth-century window.

Lunch was as filling as the conversation that threaded it and as unfamiliar as the sights the explorers recounted. We were accustomed, even the men, to a light meal in the middle of the day, a bit of cold meat, salad, fruit perhaps or cheese and the ubiquitous Ry-Krisp. The middle-of-the-day lunch on the *St. Patrick* included soup, meat, potatoes, a vegetable sometimes, though green things were hard to come by, and a sweet for dessert. There were a few cries of startled surprise but no complaints and no waste. We excused this shamefacedly to one another by the voiced discovery we'd all been brought up by the rigid dictum, "If the plate is not clean, no dessert." We disobeyed the childhood rule only once a day. At breakfast we left on our plate the potatoes. We ate, without comment and without excuse at every meal, bread toasted, sending the baskets back again and again to be refilled. When I was a child, my grandmother's cook, Erna, used to make what she called Oven Toast. I had not forgotten it and I had not had it in all the years between until Maeve gave it to us on the *St. Patrick*. Irish bread is not the damp Kleenex-like substance we call bread at home. It has body, texture and flavor and is much the size and shape of a French loaf. For toast it is cut thick and, I think, browned in the oven, where it swells and becomes lighter in texture. I will not say that Irish toast for breakfast is better than a French *croissant* but it comes a close second and has one advantage. One can eat much more of it, even with jam or marmalade on top.

By the end of lunch, conversation had almost died away. We left the table in a blissful lethargy of indecision between settling ourselves on deck or moving the few feet into the living room where we could read, and no one was fooled for a moment by that assertion. Harvey the maverick, bristling with energy and paintbrushes, began a new watercolor. Biffy and Lloyd, gathering up binoculars on the way, took up posts on deck for bird watching. Sophy joined them for fresh air. It has been my contention over long years of friendship with Sophy that she pursues fresh air with the fervor of an Alpine traveler in search of edelweiss. For Sophy as for the Alpine traveler it is not there for the taking. You must "get" it.

Ellen barricaded herself at one end of the couch with guidebooks and maps, put on her glasses and plunged into one of these defenses. I saw this with misgiving. I, and it is not to my credit, am not a pursuer of edelweiss, fresh air or sightseeing. When I cruise, cruising is what I like to do, enjoying deeply the landscape as it comes toward me, allowing it to pass uninvestigated and another slide into its place. *In situ*, for Ellen, is a starting point from which to start her radiations by reading, map consulting, drawing up lists, marking down mileage and frequently consulting with Lloyd. He, far from compressing her plan, finds almost always other places that by stretching a bit could be included. They do not force on others these planned side excursions, they suggest, and are only a little bewildered, not displeased, when the plans are not embraced *in toto* with joy.

Albert, making himself comfortable in an armchair that faced Ellen's couch, confided to no one in particular he was very comfortable but had nothing to read and insufficient energy to fetch a book from his stateroom.

With patent eagerness and totally false shyness, I suggested, if he had nothing better, would he like to see an advance copy of my new book? Publication date was six weeks away but an advance copy had been sent to me the day before we left and I had just happened to toss it into my luggage.* Because no one except his wife Frances is so motivated by concern for other people's feelings, I knew he would not refuse my offer. I would not have heard him if he had refused. As I finished speaking I was already halfway to my cabin. He accepted the book with cries of pleasure and gratifying expressions of pride and privilege in being the first to read it. Frances was at a table opposite the one Harvey was using; she had a portfolio open and was writing. Incredulity got the better of manners and unabashedly I looked over her shoulder. From six to eight postcards, she had removed and was inscribing one. I knew from a previous cruise† the Hacketts are postcard addicts. However small the place visited, they can find a postcard in it. I know antique collectors will explore unlikely places but I doubt that they

* *Now and Then,* published November 1972.
† *Floating Island,* published October 1968

24

include butcher shops, for example, in their search. The Hacketts do. Any shop, in their opinion, might include in its stock a few cards, and experience has confirmed their opinion. Many of the treasures they acquire they send to friends. The rest they keep as *souvenirs de voyage*. I had thought this redundant because Albert always had a camera with him, even while searching for postcards, and took a great many pictures. But when he showed me his pictures of the Irish cruise, a total of three, he confided these were the only ones that had come out. The paucity was due in great part to his forgetful habit of taking many pictures with no film in the camera. Postcards filled the gap.

The reason for my incredulity and bad manners of looking over Frances' shoulder was my conviction there had not been a single moment of opportunity in place or time to find postcards. She and Albert had not gone into Killaloe. By their own admission they had stayed on the boat to unpack. I knew their genius for ferreting cards out of the most un-likely places, I told her, but she had not been in any place at all; how could she have produced them? She must have brought them from New York. That had to be the explana-tion of such a sleight-of-hand trick. She looked up at me, smiling. "Oh no, dawlin'," she protested, "these are Irish postcards." A sudden cock of the head and wider grin made her look for the instant like a mischievous and defiant child. "I found them at the airport in Shannon when we were waiting for the cars and you thought I'd gone to the ladies' room." She went back to her writing.

On my way to join the bird watchers and fresh-air breather on deck, I passed between Ellen and Albert. Ellen did not look up from her guidebooks and maps. Neither did Albert, but not from his reading. My book, that exciting first copy, was spread across his chest, open at the first page, its eager reader deep in peaceful slumber.

25

Maeve was close behind me when I came on deck, though I had not heard her, probably because I had not yet memorized the construction of the door sill that placed it a few inches above the floor on either side. The others seemed to have accommodated themselves almost immediately to the change in level. After an unintended dive or two, they evidently remembered to lift a foot at the threshold. Not remembering, I stubbed my toe, reached the deck in a spontaneous imitation of a football player about to execute a flying tackle. Maeve, righting me, pushed me gently to one side.

"I must just see to the ropes," she explained. "We're casting off."

Although we had no duties to perform, all the passengers

were wearing some form of sneakers, but not Maeve. Steadily balanced on her very high-heeled shoes, she caught a rope tossed to her from the dock, coiled it neatly over a stanchion and ran toward the stern down a narrow outside passage I would have maneuvered with difficulty and crabwise; I never tried it. She must have caught and coiled another rope there. We heard her call up to Anthony, "All free." Anthony's seat of operations in the stern was of a height to allow him, looking over the length of his boat, a full view of the water beyond. I doubt that any of those inside heard this or were aware of what was happening, but those of us on deck forward looked at one another and I will remember always a sound we made. Each of us as if on cue gave a deep sigh of fulfillment. This was the moment we had planned and come a long way for. The curtain was going up.

3

"The River Shannon," I quote from the *Encyclopaedia Britannica,* "is the principal river of Ireland. It flows with a bow-shaped course from north to south and southwest, from the northwest part of the island to its mouth in the Atlantic on the southwest coast, with a length of about 161 miles and a drainage area of 4,554 square miles." I know from other sources that a lough is a lake and I learn again from the *Encyclopaedia* it, the Shannon, forms Loughs Boderg (eight miles long) and Forbes (two miles) and Ree (eighteen miles) . . . and Lough Derg (twenty-four miles). "The Shannon pursues as far as Lough Derg a sluggish way through wide areas of lake, bog and marsh. From its exit from Lough Derg at Killaloe to tidewater at Limerick, the gradient increases ,to just over 100 feet in sixteen miles. No wholly satisfactory explanation of this change in character from a mature if not aged upper course to a youthful lower course has yet been given."

No explanation has yet been given me in any reading how

a river goes into a lake and comes out at the other side. I do understand the widening and the narrowing of a river in its course but these widenings are not called lakes. I do not see how a river can create a lake or a series of lakes and continue as a river. What part of Lough Derg and the other loughs is the river? This lack of comprehension no doubt is due to my inability to grasp the principles of geology, an inability that very nearly cost me my college degree. My understanding of the ways of the Shannon was even more muddied by being told on the authority of the captain and Mr. Kearsley that when it is a river the Shannon is a gentle tranquil body of water but when it is a lake it can be turbulent and tricky for sailors. A few minutes after our quiet departure the captain sent word by Maeve that we were now in Lough Derg, the added information of its trickiness and the luck that we were crossing it on a fine day.

The day was fine though misty at the corners of our view. Blue heron were in the marshes near the water, cattle in the fields beyond, but we saw neither houses nor people. Biffy and Lloyd with their binoculars saw a number of other birds and called to each other excitedly for mutual corroboration. Caught up by their excitement and because I love birds too, in an ignorant way, I called their attention to the ones I spotted, but since these turned out invariably to be either moorhens or gulls, and the patience of the experts seemed to be wearing thin, I let them get on without me. I did not propose my voluntary and considerate withdrawal to be unnoticed, however. If I created no further interruptions, I, suggested, would they give to me at the end of the cruise a list of the birds they had seen? The response to this proposal I considered over-enthusiastic. Nevertheless I am grateful now for their scrupulous fulfillment of the promise and I include here the list and notation Lloyd gave me.

Dear Emily:

We saw these birds along the Shannon and its fields:

Lapwings
Curlews
Moorhens (the most plentiful of the shore birds)
Coots
Mute swans (especially on Lake Ree)
Hooded crows as well as the usual carrion crows
Mallards (on the River Boyle)
Pied and white wagtails (the most plentiful of the land birds)
Gulls:
    Immature black-headed gulls (in great quantities at
      Athlone)
    Common gulls
    Lesser black-backed gulls

Shags
Gray herons
Magpies
Great crested grebe
Chaffinches (at Mount Shannon)

And one dazzlingly beautiful little kingfisher darting among the shrubs like a hummingbird with his brilliant blue-green back and russet tummy and his blue-black wings beating with incredible speed. Sophy was the first to spot him. He was tiny compared with our kingfishers but had the same thrust-forward head and long stout beak, shaped like a dagger. His little feet were bright red and his throat was white. We cheered him with joy as he whirled by us.

If you want pictures of any of these birds with which to refresh your memory I'll be glad to send you the proper Peterson.

A sailboat danced toward us out of the mist, dipping and curtsying as we passed her. It was a pretty sight that gave me double pleasure because I was watching from a sober steady barge and not cavorting about in a sailboat. I remembered at the moment a summer when my twin daughters, about twelve years old, were learning to sail. What I was remembering specifically was the day they had persuaded me to be shown their prowess. I was a less experienced sailor than they but I had convictions. I liked things including boats, I shouted, to be on an even keel. After what had seemed to me a generous portion of eternity in time, we had gradually eased out of a violent tipping and tilting to the steadiness I had been begging for. From my position forward into which terror had cemented me, I had called to my girls in the stern. Nothing would have induced me to turn so much as my head lest I upset the balance they had taken so long to accomplish.

"Now you are really sailing."

From behind, a voice heavy with exasperation reached me: "Mother, we are completely becalmed. We're rowing."

Evidence of activity brought me out of my reminiscing. Maeve was on deck and at the ropes again. Mr. Kearsley was behind her.

"We're stopping off at a little village. We won't stay long, but I thought you might like to look about. It's called Garrykennedy, but it's scarcely on the map." I do not know how a place can be scarcely on a map but I liked the image the phrase provoked of Garrykennedy peeking timidly over the edge of an atlas. The indoor workers and sleeper joined us, Albert declaring unconvincingly he'd been so immersed in my book he had forgotten where he was. He caught my eye and stopped.

Directly ahead of us, marking the harbor, rose a jagged gray stone ruin of something, of a Norman watchtower, we

32

learned, and we were to see frequently these stark reminders of invasions. I count them as symbolic of the country as the shamrock.

Garrykennedy as a village does not qualify for inclusion in a map, even scarcely, but it made a place for itself in our remembrance of travel points because on its single street we counted four pubs and saw no other shops. We walked beyond the last cottage up a dusty road that wound aimlessly between fields and since there seemed to be no terminus, we, like the King of France in the nursery rhyme, "went up the hill and then came down again."

Two or three old men were standing separately at some distance from our boat when we returned to it. Several of us called out "Good afternoon" but only a head nodded in response. We were piped, literally sung on board, however, by a roaring drunk. We had not encountered him earlier. I do not know which of the pubs had enjoyed his patronage. He called to us. The message was blurred, his tone was hearty, and he waved both arms around as if he were exercising, but actually, I think, to assist his balance. He was still waving and shouting when we left Garrykennedy; the other men had neither moved nor spoken. As we waved back to the inebriated Grover Whalen on the dock, Maeve, on the run, made her way among us, her high heels tapping a quick rhythm. If we were ready, she told us as she passed, she would like to serve tea. Tea in generous china pots was accompanied by delicious little teacakes just out of the oven. Reaching for a second one, I announced the principle I intended to follow: "I do not diet when I am on a holiday trip."

We tied up for the night at Dromineer and had our first dinner on the *St. Patrick*. Sophy, who on earlier trips had earned the title of the General, was also by her own appointment the wine steward. At Killaloe while others had been

33

stalking culture and beauty, the General had conferred with Mr. Kearsley about the wines and spirits the company would like. Mr. Kearsley had gone off in his car with her list and reported back to her he had been able to satisfy it. Between them they had also worked out a financial arrangement that was agreeable to everyone. Neither of the girls would be asked to be on duty at the bar. We would make our own drinks, which we much preferred, and would pay by the bottle. Mr. Kearsley would charge enough more than the standard price in order to allow himself a profit, but not so much as individual drinks would bring. This was for the whiskey, gin, vodka and the Cinzano the Hacketts and I drink in lieu of cocktails. The wine at dinner would be by the bottle. The bar, made up of a counter and shelves behind, was scarcely large enough to hold one person. It was at the far end of the dining area and adjoined the kitchen. Certainly there was not room there for a full supply, but we discovered the extra storage space when Maeve, dislodging occupants of the couch in the sitting room, lifted the seat; it was the lid of an ample storage chest that ran the full length of the couch.

We had changed for dinner. In the early days of talking to one another about what to bring we had been in emphatic agreement that something different from daytime wear had to be included, not necessarily a long robe or dress. Several of us preferred this, but, if short, whatever was different from the daytime sturdy tweeds. The men were just as insistent as the women about changing if only to another jacket. As one after another came upstairs we sensed an unmistakable and increasing sense of festivity. It is my conviction that change of clothes and cocktails make the happiest punctuation for the end of a day. It would head a list I might make of "travel tips."

When we were settled cozily with our drinks, Ellen gave

us a digest of what she had extracted from her afternoon reading about Dromineer. The information, she admitted, was scanty, hard to find and not quite what we had come to see. She read from Fodor's *Ireland,* "The village is noted for its amiable hospitality to visitors who are interested in any kind of water sports from fishing to swimming," and from L. T. C. Rolt's *Green and Silver,* "When it was suggested that we should stay and take part in the races of the next and last day of the regatta, we did not need much persuading."

The recollection of the sail with my twins came back again and I shuddered involuntarily. To my horrified apprehension, the others exchanged wistful speculations about the possibility of our arrival timing with a regatta. When Mary announced dinner, I had almost completely reversed my belief in the beneficent stimulation and camaraderie a cocktail provides.

At lunch each of us had been given a napkin ring with the admonishment each of us must return his napkin to it at the end of a meal. We had been obedient about this but had taken no notice of any individual markings on the ring. Lloyd's was the only one recognizable because it contained only a corner of the most flamboyant outspread and convoluted piece of napery any of us, we agreed, had ever seen. Ellen was reproachful but Lloyd defended himself.

"I never went to kindergarten," he said, "so I never learned to fold anything." He did not learn on the voyage either, though not for want of patient endeavors of instruction.

Dinner was hearty, hot and delicious, in no way reminiscent of French cuisine. Mary served; Maeve was in the kitchen but came out to ask as we were having dessert—a monumental apple tart—how many would like Irish coffee. During dinner we had applauded and toasted the General's selection of wine, and the enthusiastic show of hands responding to the suggestion of Irish coffee made my own spirits sink with a foreboding we would return to the matter of the sailing regatta and even—God forbid—be in it. On the contrary, God bless Irish coffee. It is not only delicious, it can be stimulating to good talk and dawdling, but not to activity.

That first night after a very long day talk was desultory, the pauses between lengthening to a scarcely spoken agreement that bed was indicated. Some of them may have gone back on deck for a last look and breath of air. Undoubtedly the General was among them. I was not. Going below, I found a heater glowing at the foot of the stairs. I had not noticed it before but it warmed the corridor and smelled. Neither the heat nor the smell penetrated my cabin. The difference in temperature there from the pleasant warmth upstairs and the daytime warmth outdoors was an unpleasant surprise. Though I was shivering as I undressed rapidly, I eyed dubiously the mound of blankets rising high above the neatly turned-down bed, into which had been tucked, I discovered, purring, the hot-water bottle indispensable in my list of things to take. It had been on my washstand to be filled by me with as hot water as the tap would provide when I went to bed. Maeve or Mary had done far better, probably by way of a kettle in the kitchen. Through its case the heat was close to boiling and delicious. I pushed down to the foot two of the blankets, I think there were six in all, and that is the last thing I remember.

# 4

Upstairs in the morning, sometime after eight, I went on deck, stepping over Lloyd who, full length on the floor of the living room, was doing stretching exercises. Each stateroom had a window good for air but impossible for view because it was set well above eye level. The small opening I had conceded in mine for air had not let in even a wisp of the fog that surrounded the *St. Patrick*.

For the same reason the others were as surprised as I had been. We learned at breakfast it, the fog, would delay our departure but give us a chance to explore Dromineer. If we could not depart, neither could sailboats, I sang to myself. Maeve welcomed each arrival with a "Good morning" and a recital of things offered for breakfast. The list included potatoes, but no fresh fruit, Maeve explaining it was very hard to come by. Ellen asked if she would try when she marketed next, to get prunes, explaining that she and Lloyd were very devoted to prunes for breakfast.

Albert, next to the last arrival, reported that Frances would be up shortly but found it easier to complete dressing

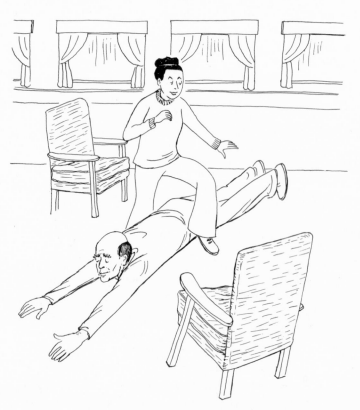

by getting him out of the way. Maeve, hearing his voice, came out from her kitchen with her "Good morning" and recited the menu. Albert, making his choice, added, "The lady I'm with would like just orange juice and Sanka, which we have brought, so if you could give us just a pot of hot water."

Maeve backed away to the kitchen, her eyes widening, and we rounded on Albert, urging him not to indulge in that kind of jocularity. When he protested he was only livening things up a bit but would restrain himself, I added further admonishment.

"It would be just as well," I said, "if you could also substitute another designation for your favorite. You always refer to Frances as 'the Madam.'" Albert said dubiously he would try.

A cry, not so much a cry as a hoarse yowl, broke the happy silence of eating. It was doubly startling because it was unexpected and because it came from Biffy, whose speaking voice gives a listener the deepest pleasure. To hear this discordant noise from her of all people was a shock.

Biffy was holding her jaw, her eyes were bright with tears and she was pointing down at her plate.

"I've either cracked a tooth or my jaw." Reassured, she became more articulate.

"If you see what looks like a little spot of fat, go around it, it's bone, solid bone. They must saw through it when they slice bacon." We were very careful but on other mornings someone would admit forgetfulness by a sharp cry of pain. However, no tooth nor jaw was cracked.

When we came on deck after breakfast the fog had lifted enough to go ashore and to see only a few yards away the jagged, though in the mist, soft outlines of ruins in stone, half ivy-covered and above the ivy two narrow openings that might have been windows or emplacements for guns, if this had once been a fortress. Since the guidebooks in their enthusiasm for the sporting opportunities of Dromineer are indifferent to this landmark, I do not know what it once was but its romantic beauty rising from the mist sent Harvey to his watercolors; the rest of us, like the fog, drifted off in irregular clumps. I went alone along the shore of the lake. By a perversity that could have been conjured up by the "little people" themselves, and I'm not at all sure it was not, I was the only one who saw the row of boathouses and boat clubs, the name of each of these inscribed over its doorway that, opened, revealed racks of boat hulls. From

39

each of these doorways a broad ramp sloped to the water and in front of almost all of these clubhouses I saw a sort of handcart on which I suppose the craft was trundled down the ramp to the water. I am probably inaccurate about a good deal of this and the only reason I mention it at all is the opportunity it gives me to vent on paper my indignation at being the only one in our company of sailors to have my sightseeing lead me to a view of the objects of a sport I thoroughly dislike. Hurrying past these, I rounded a bend and stopped at the sight of what looked in the mist like a soft white cloud on the surface of the water. I moved slowly down to the water's edge. The mist lifted; I saw a cloud of swans, and was mollified. There might have been a hundred in that nebula, I did not try to count but I shall not forget the unearthly silence and whiteness in slow motion.

When I had retraced my steps enough so that the *St. Patrick* was in sight again to use as a center, I tried another radius. I had not gone far beyond the ruins when I saw a few feet ahead a familiar rump. During a cruise on canals in England,* the General as wine steward had found it necessary every day while we were at lunch to fetch on hand and knees from a cupboard beneath the tables, beer that was stored there. It never was requested by the men until we were well into the meal. This had prompted Dorothy Stickney, a crew member, to compose a birthday message to our steward that read,

> Sophy's rear beneath the table
> Makes us think of Betty Grable.

It was Sophy's, the General's, the wine steward's rear I saw ahead of me and followed up over a crumbling stile half overgrown with vines and weeds. The General's area of

* *And a Right Good Crew.*

efficiency and competence is so wide it is comforting to find a small margin of error. Spelling is hers. Once in a Scrabble game with her I challenged a word she had spelled u-k-a. She defended it with lofty exasperation. "Have you never heard of that card game?" she inquired. "When I heard of it," I told her, "it was spelled e-u-c-h-r-e."

In the album of remarkable and beautiful photographs she has made of the cruise on the *St. Patrick* there is one that is captioned "Style into Churchyard." I think to go into a churchyard with style carries far more distinction than clambering into it over a s-t-i-l-e.

The churchyard was old, the stones choked with weeds but there was quiet charm and late wildflowers were blooming. Later, in the animated talk, during pre-luncheon apéritifs, of things seen, Frances contributed triumphantly, "I found postcards."

Harvey had not left the boat but what he had done for all of us to remember Dromineer by and to cherish for itself was a watercolor of the ruin emerging from the mist.

We were having lunch when the *St. Patrick* slipped away. The fog had left us earlier, so had Captain Anthony "for a jar," Maeve had said. Hearing this word for the second time, I asked what kind of jars Anthony had to fetch. Were they for Maeve's needs? Maeve's laughter nearly choked her. "Only Anthony's needs," she told me when she could speak. "A jar is a Guinness, or whatever he goes for at the pub. It's him I'll be fetching. I'll be back in a twink, for the pubs here are very close together."

After lunch, as hearty as the one the day before, Harvey went immediately to the table we were now referring to as his "atelier." Frances, assuring herself anxiously that no one else wanted it, took a table opposite, spreading postcards on its surface.

Albert settled himself in the chair he had occupied the day

42

before and with a book, but not mine. I would let another author, not present, be the sleep inducer. The bird watchers, the General and I went straight on deck. Ellen came and went like a dragonfly, enjoying the actual landscape unfolding, and darting back to her books and maps to verify what she was seeing and make sure she had not overlooked something of importance that might have been picked up with

Lloyd's binoculars. Once Mr. Kearsley came along the narrow outside passage to tell us we would be going from Lough Derg back into the Shannon by way of a swinging bridge at Portumna and a lock. Shortly after he had gone back to his quarters somewhere in the stern, the dragonfly visited us.

"I've just discovered," she told us, "we are going through a swinging bridge at a place called Portumna and then we

43

will go through a lock. It will be fascinating. I think I'd better alert the others."

We reached the swinging bridge at Portumna two and a half hours later. The sitting-room occupants had long since gone back to their separate occupations. Had we not opened the doors and halloed to them from the deck, they, including Ellen, would have missed it, Ellen explaining defensively she had just discovered in the guidebook a fascinating castle not far from Banagher that certainly we must visit—when we reached that place.

For those of us on deck the two and a half hours had been a time of quiet beauty not to be forgotten. We had talked very little. I remember saying when the Irish talked of a "soft" day it was *"le mot juste."* Soft was the only word that could fit the quality of the air. I had never felt anything like it and when I said felt, I meant just that. It was as tangible as if you were feeling in your fingers a piece of material like velvet. It was chilly enough to warrant wrapping a coat or a blanket around the legs but there was no sharpness. I did not say all that. I would have been rounded on for talking so much, but that was how the afternoon was for me, watching a landscape of round hills in the distance, green fields close by and rushes whispering and sighing along the water's edge.

Everyone came out to watch the bridge swing wide for us and a few minutes after, Maeve joined us, and Mr. Kearsley. We were going into a lock and both of them were needed to handle the ropes and drop overboard the padded weights that would protect our boat from scraping the wall of the lock as the water rose. I knew the requirements well, and gloated over having no part in them. Maeve was everywhere, quick and competent, tossing a coiled rope up to the lock-keeper as if she were playing deck tennis. Sophy, catching my eye at one of the maneuvers, grinned and I knew she was remembering, as I was, the time I had thrown a line to a lockkeeper. I had thrown it as if I were skipping rope and when after two or three falls into the water it had finally reached him it had also laid across his cheek a dank length of seaweed.

Returning along the outside passage to her kitchen Maeve called to us:

"I've tea ready and the cakes are just coming out of the oven."

We were glad to come indoors; the air, still soft, had grown markedly colder.

Mr. Kearsley had said we should reach Banagher at about six o'clock. Wanting to see our arrival there, we had not gone below to change for dinner. At Killaloe we had found the *St. Patrick* tied up along a stone quay. At Dromineer we had pulled in to a wood dock. The landing at Banagher was different. We might have been driving along a highway and turned off into a side road. We came under a long bridge I walked across the next day, immediately turned right into a backwater and stopped along a bank. Mr. Kearsley jumped ashore, took a rope from Maeve, carried it around a spike driven in the grass, and repeated this at the stern. Maeve at the bow moved, from the rail where it had been leaning, what might have been a deck chair in size and appearance, but turned out to be a folding gangplank. She pushed it toward Mr. Kearsley, who, catching the end extended, set it firmly pressed down, on the ground. A groove on the underside at Maeve's end accommodated exactly the sill of the deck. Mr. Kearsley returned to the boat by way of a firm gangplank. The General who likes things to tally looked at her watch. With the satisfaction of one who single-handed has accomplished a difficult feat, she announced, "It's exactly six o'clock."

Mr. Kearsley on his way to the stern looked back, visibly

45

startled. "Did you say six o'clock? Surely it must be at least half past," he added hopefully.

The General shook her head. "I set my watch by my radio this morning. But you said we'd be here at six o'clock. You and Anthony must be very pleased."

Mr. Kearsley shook his head and there was sorrow in the gesture. "I'll tell Anthony. He'll be dumbfounded too. We were sure it would be close to seven. Counted on it."

When he was out of sight, Sophy looked from one to the other of us. "Have you ever in your life heard anything so confusing? They *wanted* to be late."

"Irish, dear," was Biffy's answer.

Directly ahead of the boat we saw a large and yellow meadow on which boys were playing ball. This may have been a little islet. I could not see the far end of it but on its far side there was evidently water because I could see a number of little boats tied up. Along our shore a dusty lane straggled unevenly up a hill to what must have been a main road from the number of cars going and coming across the bridge. From the deck we could see a heavy base of old worn stone that obviously supported a building. A path leading uphill somewhere and old stone were evocative enough for me on the instant to say aloud, a bit of exploring was indicated. When my feet were on the gangplank, the General reminded us dinner would be at seven. I turned back, agreeing with Biffy's proposal that we change our clothes now and walk after dinner.

At some time during the meat—and certainly potatoes—course, Lloyd tapped with a spoon on his wineglass.

"Ellen has something to tell us," he announced.

Ellen was protesting before he had finished. "Oh, Lloyd, what do you mean? I haven't got anything to tell, I mean it isn't a speech. You really shouldn't say such things." She took a deep breath. "Well," she exhaled it, "it's only that, although Lloyd really shouldn't have—I did happen to find in the guidebook I was glancing through this afternoon" (Ellen's glancing, we knew, had taken the better part of two afternoons), "I did see and then I thought I ought to make sure and so I looked in other guidebooks and it really is there, so I thought if it would be possible tomorrow because I think we could get there in about half an hour. Of course, we would need two cars but that wouldn't take any longer if they went at the same time, would it? Of course, if we have to leave right on the dot of something then we couldn't do it."

"There are no dots on this trip," Biffy interrupted her. "We're learning that."

The General took advantage of the interruption. "I'm all for it," she declared. "I would only like to know what it is we'll see, if that's not being too inquisitive."

"Why, my dear," Ellen answered, "as I have been saying, I think we should see Birr." Since this was the first time any of us, except Lloyd, had heard the name, several of us echoed it.

Ellen was a little impatient with us. "My dears," she said, "of course, you must know Birr Castle and the Earl of Rosse, the famous astronomer, only of course it's the gardens we want to see and the Earl of Rosse is married to the mother of Lord Snowden, only not the same one, of course, I mean not the astronomer Earl of Rosse."

Here was a project to stir the General's blood. Undoubtedly there was something very worthwhile to see if Ellen was recommending it, but it demanded organization, and that was the icing on the cake. Cars must be engaged, the route mapped out, the distance calculated, the company divided between two cars and the time scheduled, calculated, and set down. She patted Ellen's arm affectionately.

She was conferring with Mr. Kearsley and Maeve when I

left the boat and climbed the path to the top of the hill. My conjecture had been right. The path came out on obviously a main road. To the right was the long bridge under which we had passed to reach the backwater. The village must be to the left. I walked along the one road, seeing no side lanes in either direction and I looked into the windows of shops long since closed.

Later, at home, I read in a book on Ireland a description of Banagher: "The little town wanders up a gentle slope in a single wide main street." I found that street very poorly lit, but even in the darkness, interspersed among the shops, I saw several houses that seemed to me to have both substance and style. I doubt he lived in one of these, the young man of twenty-six who came in 1841 to fill the post of clerk to the district surveyor. His name was Anthony Trollope. He lived ten years in Banagher and began his writing there.

At the top of the hill the street was better lighted than it had been where I joined it from the path, and evidently some of the shops were open because I saw Frances and Albert coming out of one. They saw me at the same time and waved, more in triumph than in greeting.

"Postcards," Frances called, before I could reach them. I was not bowled over with astonishment at the news, I told them, and was even more offensive by offering to bet I could name the reason for Albert's jubilation. He immediately took me up on it. For one of America's most distinguished playwrights, Albert Hackett is astonishingly ingenuous at times. This was one of them.

"Ice cream," I said.

Although his usual expression is one of surprise at practically everything, his eyes widened to amazement and he pursed his lips for whistling.

"Oh my, you hit it. I owe you a shilling, but let me get you some ice cream too. It's pretty good. Of course, nothing like the French ice cream."

From an earlier trip* I have learned that for Albert there is nothing in the world comparable in enjoyment to eating French ice cream. I know only one other such pinnacle of delight and that was Rat's in *The Wind in the Willows*. He said, "There is *nothing*—absolutely nothing—half so much worth doing as simply messing about in boats . . . or *with* boats. . . . In or out of 'em, it doesn't matter." I never think of Albert and French ice cream without remembering about Rat. I declined with thanks his invitation. Unlike Albert or Rat, I cannot reduce to one the sources of my enjoyment. They include ice cream, but not messing about in boats. I would accept the shilling, however, I reminded him, and the transaction was immediately completed.

We strolled back down the hill together but stopped simultaneously, asking one another if it were possible we had gone off the main road. We were staring at festoons of lights in trees along a narrow lane that separated two cottages. All this area had been dark when each of us left the *St. Patrick*. There had only been flickering streetlights at wide intervals up the hill. Now at the end of this lane we saw a considerable open space. As we stood gaping, a small truck turned from the road into this lane and very slowly made the passage without touching the cottage on either side. There were five or six men riding in the cramped space of the cab. They jumped down and unloaded from its back, wooden flooring in sections. They laid this on the ground. Crosspieces of supports underneath gave it a height of perhaps eight to ten inches. The sections fitted together evenly and were evidently in a specific order because I heard the men calling out numbers to one another. When the floor was down, one man drove the truck to a far corner of the field. His companions stood about and presently he rejoined them. We asked them what was going on. They told us, " 'T

* *Floating Island.*

49

will be a dance." Another truck came up the lane. A platform was unloaded and, set up, was a good eight or more feet high. This was the platform for the musicians, the height enabling the players to look down on the dancers. Now people were hurrying up the lane in couples and groups. Suddenly a spotlight, installed in one of the trees, blazed out over the stage and a good portion of the surrounding neighborhood. We were caught in it and so were Maeve and Mary, running up the path from the boat. We knew then we had not wandered off the road. We stopped the girls, promising we would hold them only a minute or two but were bursting with questions to ask.

They were in no hurry, they told us, the dancing probably would not get under way until around about eleven or half past and it was scarcely ten now. This was a traveling dance orchestra with its own dance platform and Mary said, "They raise a tent over it if the weather's bad. They put up posters ahead of time and everybody comes from nearby." Mostly a couple of girls or a group of them would come as one party and the same with the boys. "Then you pretty much dance with anybody after things really get started, but a girl doesn't come with a fella unless she's definitely walking out with him."

The musicians were tuning up. Maeve's feet and Mary's too were tapping. We said good night and they ran.

No one was on deck nor visible indoors when we returned to the *St. Patrick.* Harvey's table studio seemed closed for the night. We sat on deck for a little while listening to the music and watching the lights and shadows on the river. When we went indoors and below, we were saying how picturesque it all was, what charm in the traveling dance.

At two thirty in the morning, the music of the traveling dance had lost its charm for me; I was consigning it to the bottom of the river and even to lower depths.

# 5

Biffy and Harvey were the last ones up to breakfast next morning. I was giving, unasked, my opinion of music that went on some four hours and not once during that time vouchsafed so much as a fragment of a tune. Nothing but boom, boom, pound, pound. At the moment I caught sight of Biffy and Harvey they were looking at each other quizzically. I stopped my diatribe. I knew or guessed the meaning of that look. Without even waiting to make a bet I said:

"You went to that dance last night." My assertion was not based on unfounded inspiration. Harvey has the uncontested tribute paid to him of being one of the best dancers in the City of New York and the State of Connecticut, and Biffy is his match. They admitted delightedly my clairvoyance.

"I've never had a better time," Biffy asserted.

"She certainly never lacked for partners," Harvey contributed. "Nor did I, come to think of it," he added. "You couldn't find friendlier people. They treated us as if we belonged in the neighborhood. I hope we run into another one." It was a hope I did not share.

The appearance of Mr. Kearsley checked an announcement of this hope. Mr. Kearsley, I had begun to realize,
always appeared. He never came into a room or along the
deck to join us. He had a Cheshire Cat gift for "fade-ins"
and "fade-outs," as they say in Hollywood. Now, smiling
diffidently, he made me aware he was among us. There was
nothing furtive about his coming and going. It was rather
a kind of magic. He suggested, that morning, places, people
and things in and around Banagher.

Up the hill and across the road from where the *St. Patrick*
was moored, we learned, there was a shop for Irish home
industries. It was run by two English ladies to whom he
had telephoned. Though the season was over and the shop
closed, they would be happy, they said, to open it and receive
us if we liked. We would find there tweeds, woolens and a
variety of handicrafts. Our enthusiastic acceptance seemed to
give him further confidence. Would we then, he wondered
apologetically, like to drive to Birr Castle, the seat of the
Earl of Rosse? We would go in two cars he would order and
be back for lunch. "The gardens are nice" was the conclusion of his sales talk. Mr. Kearsley would never have
qualified as a representative of the Fuller Brush Company.

We offered no sales resistance. Thanks to Ellen we knew
about Birr Castle, but the moment he had said the word
"Birr," Ellen had ejaculated in my ear a phrase I strongly
doubted I was hearing correctly. My attention was on Mr.
Kearsley. She repeated the phrase, however, and in mounting emphasis on her part and mounting incredulity on mine.
The instant Mr. Kearsley stopped speaking she flung it at
the group and I was reassured to see on their faces an echo
of my surprise.

"Umbilicus Hiberniae," is what she said and had been
saying. After a few comments I do not choose to repeat, she
was allowed to continue.

"If you weren't so ignorant as well as vulgar and if you read guidebooks now and then instead of mooning on deck over the view, though Biffy and Lloyd are of course wonderful about birds and of course it *is* very important to know about the birds where you're traveling and you do have a much better chance to observe them from a boat than if you were motoring, slower and quieter—"

Lloyd so enjoys Ellen's circumlocutions, he is unwilling to stem them. The General likes a direct route.

"Tell us about the Umbilicus," she suggested. Ellen obliged.

"That's what a man named Sir William Petty called the village of Birr, 'Umbilicus Hiberniae.' He was a surveyor in the seventeenth century and he said Birr was the center of Ireland, only it was called Parsontown after Laurence Parsons who owned the estates surrounding it. A descendant of his was made Earl of Rosse. That doesn't quite explain 'Birr,' does it?" She paused to consider this. "However, Petty wrote it in his *Survey of Ireland.* I've just been reading all about it. I've been dying to go but some of you"— looking directly at me—"said I was not to keep suggesting side trips and places to see that took us away from the boat. We mustn't be restless to get away, we must enjoy what we see from the boat, and I am enjoying it, I love it, only I thought perhaps Lloyd and I could sneak away because we do love seeing things, I mean places as well as birds but now—"

Mr. Kearsley reappeared. I realized at some time while Ellen was talking, he had faded away.

"The ladies are waiting at the shop," he told us, "if you would care to come now. The cars will be here in an hour for the trip to Birr."

That morning before breakfast I had taken a walk across the long bridge under which we had come the afternoon before. I had stopped to enjoy directly across the main road from our mooring a low building of gray stone with a walled courtyard in front, an arched iron gate at its entrance. This was where Mr. Kearsley led us. Two women stood in the doorway at the far end of the courtyard. They were tall, wore tweeds and were smiling cordially. Their welcome was genuine and not intrusive; things were not thrust upon us and we were made to feel no obligation to make worthwhile their opening the shop for us. The rooms—there were four or perhaps five of varying sizes—contained attractively displayed Irish craft that included heavy sweaters, soft home-spun blankets or "throws" in delectable colors, scarves, ties—as a Greek friend is fond of saying, "Everything what you can imagine," including ceramics and some furniture.

Let no man in my hearing ever again speak in a derogatory way about women shoppers. The preening and prancing that went on among the men in our group reduced us to a chorus of admiring handmaidens. Sweaters were held up in front of manly chests for our enthusiastic approval. Ties were tucked under chins. Did we like this blend of color better? or that one? or that one? or that one? Long broad woven strips that we were told were called "crios" and used by fishermen in lieu of belts, were seized, wrapped round like cummerbunds and displayed for our applause. I think Frances bought a little knitted woolen hat and I think she had to do it quickly and surreptitiously so that her attention would not seem to have been distracted for a moment.

After what she considered a generous allowance of time, the General was restive. Importuned to give a decisive vote of nattiness between a tie of blended blues and grays and one of tans and orange, she said firmly she thought perhaps we'd better move on. Ellen echoed this sentiment gratefully. I had an uncomfortable feeling she had been cowed by my early insistence on not rushing about to see things. The

54

General is never cowed. Catching sight of Mr. Kearsley's sudden appearance in the doorway, they turned to him eagerly for corroboration, asking simultaneously if we should not be on our way. Mr. Kearsley's answer, though we did not recognize it at the moment, was the keynote of the whole cruise, of the Irish pattern of living, and of the subtle message of the landscape itself.

"Time enough," he said. "Time enough."

Birr Castle, as Ellen had told us, is the seat of the Earl of Rosse and he is in turn stepfather to the Earl of Snowden. The castle is a scant half-hour's drive from Banagher. The gardens are open every day to the public. Though we were not in October seeing them at their peak of bloom, we would not have allowed a gardener to finish that invariable pronouncement gardeners make, "If you had only come . . ." because they were beautiful.

Apart from full summer bloom the only sight that eluded me was of a gardener. Over all the acreage I walked, and at the end of an hour I had explored only a small part of the estate, the gatekeeper was the only person I saw. I skirted ponds, I crossed bridges over singing brooks, I followed well-marked paths through a heavily wooded park, the trees meticulously labeled both by name and source.

We had separated the moment divergent paths were indicated. Our pattern of independence was already established. If there were others in the wooded park I did not hear them. The only sound was the foolish giggling of the stream. I was enjoying a pleasantly shivery fantasy of walking through a forest in a dream, when almost at my feet, with a sound such as an alarm clock makes just before it rings, a pheasant fanning my face with its wings flew over my head. I have never come so rapidly out of a fantasy. Of all the inadequate responses to having the living daylights scared out of a body, mine, I think, takes the cake. "Gee whiz," I said. "Gee whiz." I do not remember under what circumstances I last used that expression but I am reasonably sure I was about ten years old.

Thoroughly shaken out of fantasy, I moved on through the park. Every few yards ahead and on either side of me, pheasants rose and fled but they kept their distance or perhaps I kept mine. Out of the park I followed an avenue of box hedges, "the tallest in the world and 200 years old," I read later. I read, too, that the trees in the water garden— the River Camcor flowed beside it—were imported from western China. I recognized the high and almost solid wall making its border was magnolia though certainly it was not in bloom.

Going down broad shallow stone steps that led to a series of gardens, I saw Ellen and Lloyd at the far end. Before I had reached them I knew by their gestures they were talking about the impossible size of the yew or box hedge that set off each of the gardens I had passed. We went on together past greenhouses and brick walls almost covered by an embroidery of espaliered trees. At the far end of one of these we saw a man digging. When simultaneously we pointed him out to one another we realized and said aloud how conscious we had been of the absence of gardeners, of any people working. All that land groomed and labeled had given each of us an eerie sense of unreality. Ellen suggested perhaps all the outdoor staff had gone to lunch. Ellen likes to visualize people being well taken care of. Lloyd and I thought it unlikely they had all gone at the same time. He suggested perhaps they worked seasonally or came from the village on odd days. We considered asking the man who was digging—that is, Ellen considered it. She would, she suggested, go to the man and inquire simply, "Where is everybody?" I said the man would probably consider her daft, but when Ellen answered she didn't in the least mind that, or she might say,

"Are you alone here?", we persuaded her instead to move on with us.* We were still talking about it in a desultory way as we walked, framing inquiries that might sound sensible and discarding them. We stopped walking and talking as suddenly as if a military command to halt had been shouted at us. We were looking at a miniature crenellated fortress. It might have been a playhouse or fort for a small boy except that a large telescope emerged from it. Lloyd and I gaped at this incongruity, set in the midst of gardens, park and streams and pointing nowhere. Ellen looked at us pityingly and shook her head.

"You don't read guidebooks," she said, more in reproach than sorrow. I deserved it. I am not a conscientious sightseer. I am an enthusiastic traveler but I go ill-prepared or not prepared at all for what I am going to see. Childish as this is I have never outgrown pleasure in a surprise. I like winding roads, walled gardens and rooms with doors. On a trip I like to see as much as possible without undue effort along the way. My purpose is not to verify what I have previously read. Had I known that at Birr I would see the telescope invented by and constructed under the supervision of an Earl of Rosse, I would have been cheated of the pleasure of astonishment. Now I know more about Birr and the Earls of Rosse because I have read, as I like to read, after seeing. For me, pre-reading creates a jumble, post-reading a clarifying and a stamping in my memory.

The scientist-astronomer, I can now report, was the third Earl of Rosse. There is no evidence of accomplishment or even interest in science until the third Earl, who without a

* Perhaps I found an explanation in the happy discovery of *Akenfield: Portrait of an English Village* by Ronald Blythe (Penguin Books, 1972) in which he quotes a conversation with a gardener on a big estate: "We must never be seen from the house; it was forbidden. And if people were sitting on the terrace or on the lawn, and you had a great barrow-load of weeds, you might have to push it as much as a mile to keep out of view."

conventional background of academic degrees designed and supervised the building on the estate, of what was to be for seventy years the largest telescope in the world.

The "Turbina" is not preserved at Birr, though its debut was more dramatic than the telescope. The "Turbina" was the first vessel with a turbine engine. It was invented by and built under the supervision of the fourth Earl of Rosse. Disgruntled by the Navy's lack of interest and with an added dash of inventiveness, he took the boat to Cowes at the time of Queen Victoria's Diamond Jubilee celebration. Inasmuch as craft of very nearly every description from very nearly every part of the world had assembled there, this one caused no particular interest until one day when a stately flotilla was on parade, an outlandish boat appeared seemingly from nowhere and, darting impudently in and about the scandalized dowager ships, shot ahead of the leader and out of sight. Considerable attention was paid to it that day and thereafter by the Navy.

Dramatically and perhaps geographically the telescope is a central point at Birr Castle; for me it was a terminal one. I had seen enough, my limit of absorption had been reached, and my legs were tired. My underpinnings will carry me staunchly over a length of time and area if I am walking; they crumple after a relatively short period of standing. True, at Birr I had walked, but I had also stood to enjoy details, then walked, then stood again. At the moment when my legs cried "Enough," I doubted I would have gone a quarter of a mile farther to see one of the Seven Wonders of the World.

That is not Ellen's pattern; therefore she has seen a great deal more of the world than I will ever set my legs to discovering. No wonder I was astonished to hear her say to my announcement that the telescope was my terminus:

"I'll go back with you. I think we've seen everything."

Lloyd accepted this for Ellen and me, not for himself. He

would wander a little farther, find the others of our company and return with them.

Ellen and I found Frances and Albert at the entrance gate. Ellen was uneasy.

"I should have gone with Lloyd," she said, "he may see something."

She was in distress at the discovery, when we had reassembled on the *St. Patrick,* there were parts of the garden she had not seen. She does not ever knowingly commit a sin of omission. It was difficult to determine from her cries of dismay whether she was troubled by her own omission or the discovery that Lloyd had seen something she had not.

"You know," she told him, "Mr. Kearsley said we were to be back for lunch and the cars were waiting for us and Frances and Albert were at the gate and you said you would go and find the others."

Lloyd admitted this. "And when I found them they were in a part of the garden we hadn't seen."

"I shouldn't have left," was Ellen's mournful conclusion. She turned to me. "But you said you were ready to go. Did you know we hadn't seen everything?"

"No, I didn't," I told her. I had not actually known there was more to be seen than we had covered, but I had suspected it.

Mr. Kearsley had been on deck when we returned. Seeing him, Frances had called out anxiously she hoped we were not late, she was sure the others would be following immediately. Anxiety lest she inconvenience or in some way disturb other human beings is the polestar by which her course is set. I cannot resist interpolating an example of this. Recently she has been introduced to the game of Ping-Pong and taken to it with passionate enthusiasm. The first time she played, after a series of understandably ineffectual shots, she sent a swift one impossible for her opponent to return. At once Frances put down her paddle, leaned across the net to say, with tears in her voice, "Forgive me, dawlin'."

Mr. Kearsley was obviously surprised by the anxiety in Frances' voice. He told her with assurance and some bewilderment we were not late for lunch because lunch was for whenever we wished to have it.

Ellen interposed, "What about our schedule?"

Mr. Kearsley echoed the word as if it were in a foreign language and he was hearing it for the first time. "Schedule? Oh," and there was the phrase again, "time enough for that. Time enough."

In her guidebook library, Ellen had not included *The Shannon Sailors* by Leonard Wibberley. When I came to it in my post-cruise reading, I was sorry for the first and only time I had not read a book, this book, before our trip, not only because it is a delight from first to last page but because it is the most clarifying and reassuring postulate of time I have ever found. Since a postulate demands no evidence of proof, this is the quintessence of the Irish character and way of life. I had thought, until I came to Ireland, the Greeks were people indifferent to time but there is a difference. The Greeks are superior to, disdainful of, time. The small ship, on which friends and I once traveled overnight from Piraeus to the island of Chios, reached Chios two hours ahead of schedule because the crossing had been smooth. The captain had all bells rung to alert the citizens of Chios. He was not a man to be held down by schedule and if any of them wished to take his boat they'd better bestir themselves. He had no intention of waiting about until time caught up with him.

Now there is no arrogance in the Irish point of view. This is what Mr. Wibberley, a dear man, I'm sure, certainly a lovely writer, says:

"I really believe that the Irish are the least anxious people in the world. There is no secret either to this absence of anxiety on their part. It lies in the realization that man lives in eternity, and time therefore is an illusion which is not to be taken seriously. There is no one in Ireland, in my experience, who attaches any importance to time, while everyone, I believe, has a strong sense of eternity. Time and eternity are, of course, the opposites of each other, so if you believe in the one you cannot take the other seriously. Not taking time seriously dissolves the greater portion of frets and worries in this world. I recommend the attitude if you are harassed in your daily life."

We spent a good part of lunch soothing Ellen over her sin of omission, Maeve urging us to relax and enjoy our food. Harvey was the only one a little impatient to get through with it because, he admitted, he was in a hurry to get across the aisle to his studio in order to set down, while they were sharp in his memory, things he had seen during the morning. When Albert with misguided generosity offered to show him postcards—no one else had seen any indication of where postcards might be purchased—Harvey declined courteously, though with, it seemed to me, a slight shudder. Albert must have been aware of it too because he added quickly and apologetically, certainly he had not thought of their being models, only reminders. At the look on Harvey's face, and there was no mistaking the purport of this, Albert's amendment and amplification died. He went with Frances to a desk where they settled to a discussion of friends to whom the cards should be addressed.

Ellen settled into what was by then her own corner of the couch, guidebooks piled around her. Biffy and Lloyd went on deck to look for birds. Sophy made herself comfortable with a book and a deck chair. I stood in the bow with no purpose in mind but enjoyment of the soft landscape, of the stillness so nearly absolute I could hear the rushes whispering along the bank as our wake reached them. There was a little mist, just enough to soften outlines of what seemed to be small towers, single shafts of what might be stone, on a hilltop to our right. It might be the island of Avalon, I thought, where King Arthur was carried to heal him of his wounds. Some say he never returned from there. No one else seemed to be aware of it, certainly no one was calling attention to it. I wondered hopefully if I might have been singled out as having special kinship with Ireland and been given second sight. If this had happened I would keep it to myself.

Ellen came on deck.

"We should be getting to Clonmacnoise shortly. Oh, there it is. Look, everybody, there's Clonmacnoise on the right. We're going to stop there, Mr. Kearsley told me this morning. That's why I came back so promptly for lunch," she added, but charitably did not complete it with, "and didn't see everything."

Everyone was staring. The Hacketts came on the run, Harvey following, paintbrush in his hand. I was staring, inversely, at myself because Ellen's announcement had jolted me out of my fantasy and into an uneasiness about what Ireland was doing to me. Of all the people I know, I have considered myself the most insensitive to "atmosphere." When others feel things in the air, I am able, try as I will, to be aware only of heat, cold or, more tangibly, rain or snow. No one else seemed to be . . . Here I was carrying on, mercifully to myself, about magic islands and second sight. I would try not to allow such daftness again, simultaneously recognizing how happy I was that it had occurred. One sentence from a guidebook would have knocked into reality that vision nothing can ever take away from my memory.

Now I know that Clonmacnoise, today a group of ruins, was founded about the year 548 by the "gentle loving tenderhearted" St. Kieran. The site was given him by King Dermott. I do not know who King Dermott was. The name Clonmacnoise means "meadow of the sons of Nos," and I do not know who Nos was. An abbey was built here. It became known for its learning throughout Europe. Monks, clerics, anchorites, bishops, scholars and students flocked to the holy place and, with the Abbot and his staff and several hundreds of tenants and workers, formed a large community. Clonmacnoise became, in fact, a great monastic city and medieval university. It was not for long, however, a sanctuary, an oasis of serenity in a troubled world. It was instead a victim of plundering, burning and invasion many times by Vikings, the "Anglo-Normans" and the English. It was almost destroyed in 1552 and that was a thousand years after its beginning. This destruction was by the English garrison at Athlone. When the churches were partially restored, Cromwell's men leveled them again. The poem I found in a little souvenir booklet in Athlone carries in its simplicity, I think, the history of Clonmacnoise and its epitaph.

### The Dead at Clonmacnois*
by T. W. Rolleston
*(from the Irish of Angus O'Gillan)*

In a quiet watered land of roses
    Stands Saint Kieran's city fair;
And the warriors of Erin in their famous generations
    Slumber there.

There beneath the dewy hillside sleep the noblest
    Of the clan of Conn,
Each below his stone with name in branching Ogham
    And the sacred knot thereon.

* Variation in spelling: sometimes with final e, sometimes without.

There they laid the seven kings of Tara,
  There the sons of Cairbre sleep—
Battle-banners of the Gael in Kieran's plain of crosses
  Now their final hosting keep.

And at Clonmacnois they laid the men of Teffia,
  And right many a lord of Breagh;
Deep the sod above Clan Creide and Clan Conaill
  Kind in hall and fierce in fray.

Many and many a son of Conn the Hundred-fighter
  In the red earth lies at rest;
Many a blue eye of Clan Colman the turf covers
  Many a swan-white breast.

We tied up at a diminutive dock. As we stepped ashore to bright green meadows soft underfoot, Captain Anthony from the bridge called down, "You're walking now in County Offaly." A path at the far end of the meadow led us up a hill. At its top we climbed over a stile of rough stones, discovering to our astonishment on the far side of the wall a broad paved highway carrying considerable motor traffic. We turned away quickly and climbed down into the past. Reaching it, we separated.

Sometimes I would be aware of two or three companions moving slowly along a wall of grave slabs or looking up at one of the great crosses, bending over gravestones in the grass, walking along a path that ran between the slabs, standing before tombstones, each one topped with an ancient rounded Celtic cross. I do not remember that we spoke to one another; I remember vividly the silence of our wonder. No one called out, "Come and look at this one." I think someone suggested, probably the General, that we ought to be getting back to the boat. We could see figures standing on the dock but they were not waving us to come. They looked relaxed and so I went down the hill only when my legs

were tired of standing. Ellen understandably was the last, and from her look of happy serenity I knew she had not been guilty of a sin of omission.

It is a heady moment when someone born in Indiana is asked to explain a detail of navigation to natives of the Eastern seaboard. Biffy, Harvey and I were the only ones on deck. When Biffy called out suddenly, "What in the world is that?" and Harvey answered, "I don't know," I liked to died.

"Why that, dears," I told them, "is a weir. We must be through a lock soon. Would you like me to tell you what a weir is?" If I sounded offensive, I did not, in my intoxication, care atall, atall. "Evidently the river here is too shallow to carry us through, so they've built a lock and alongside of it the weir, that is a dammed area to hold and raise the water level."

They were kind to me.

"We do know about locks and weirs," Harvey admitted quite apologetically. "I just hadn't recognized this one."

"I'd never heard of either," I acknowledged, "until I cruised on canals in England. Ever since then, I can't resist showing off."

Certainly we stayed on deck to watch Maeve, as steadily balanced on her high-heeled shoes as a ballet dancer on her "points," toss a rope up to the lockkeeper standing well over a man's height above us. The distance lessened as the flood of water rushing in pushed us up from beneath as if we were on a rather old-fashioned shaky elevator until we were on a level with the cobblestoned quay and, one at a time, taking the outstretched hand of the lockkeeper, stepping ashore for a moment.

On the shore side of the quay we saw a row of what looked to be warehouses and were. Ahead of us was a long bridge across the Shannon and beyond the warehouses a provoca-

tive narrow road that going uphill rounding a corner led
—the lockkeeper answered my query—to the bridge and that
was the way to the town proper of Athlone in Westmeath.
We would follow that road in the morning, we told one
another, but after the long day just ended it did not beckon
to an evening stroll.

# 6

The things I saw next morning on my walk up the winding road, across the bridge and through the town were not listed in the books I read later; I found them interesting. Just around the curve of that beckoning road, I came to and stopped in front of a hotel. The hotel advertised bed and breakfast but what had caught my happy attention was a large key at the end of a long silver chain that was, by means of a metal plate, attached to one side of the door-frame. Above the frame, on a card, was the request and invitation to unlock the door and come in. I apologize to the Irish for wondering why leaving the door unlocked would not have been a simpler way. It would not have been the Irish way of hospitality. I counted thirty-nine pubs on the main street in Athlone, another evidence of Irish hospitality. I stopped to read several times a large sign outside the movie theater. I found it confusing but concluded it was a sign of Irish independence and freedom of choice among days and dates, with a shrug to the calendar. I read:

A little farther on I joined Frances and Albert at a shop-window. They suggested I join them in pointing out, in order to remember, the range of displays. In spite of this combined effort I think we overlooked some merchandise. It included fishing tackle, Irish towels, souvenir postcards and curios, a delicate china tea set, some items of hardware, Irish silver candlesticks, samples of flatware and beautiful pieces of Waterford glass. Frances and Albert moved on but I went into the shop and bought one of the Waterford pieces, a charming bowl. I had it shipped direct from the shop for a wedding present to a cousin. It arrived in good time and in several hundred small pieces. The purchase money was cheerfully refunded and I found and sent a replacement in Waterford glass at Altman's in New York.

At the end of the long main street I read a sign swinging from a small hostelry: CYCLISTS REST. TEA SERVED. Without the possessive apostrophe this became an order, at least a suggestion, for pedestrians, too, so I complied with it. No one was in the pleasant room I walked into. It faced the street, had a large fireplace halfway down its length, and a table set for four in front of the hearth. There was a table in front of each of two windows. The lady who came through a door at the far end of the room was very tall, with lively blue eyes, short crisp gray hair and a wide smile. She did not ask what I wanted. Tea would be "to your hand in a twink," she said.

Stooping over, she touched a match to a small fire laid, and swung over it a teakettle on a hob. While we waited for the water to boil she asked where I came from, how many children I had and did I know her cousin Rory Clancy in Boston? She echoed the regretful shake of my head.

"You'll meet him surely the next time you're there. Tell him his cousin Agatha was speaking of him."

The tea, I thought with my first swallow and gasp, might have stood alone without support of the pot. My hoarse but apologetic request for hot water was granted with sorrowful tolerance.

"You'll be taking the backbone out of it."

When I had drunk as little as possible without hurting her feelings, and eaten two dry "biscuits," crackers to us, I said I must move on. She was sorry, she protested, to let me go, we were having such a nice visit.

"Well," was my answer, "you've asked all about me. I'd like to know about you before I go. Tell me about your children."

My new friend threw back her head, laughing so robustly and infectiously I joined in, not knowing why.

"Holy Mother and all the saints," she managed to say and looked down at me. "I've no chick nor child. I'm an old maid. And I'll tell you this," laying a hand on my shoulder, "once you get over the disgrace, it's airier."

Traffic on the thoroughfare of Athlone was heavy. Waiting to cross it in a group of pedestrians, I watched pass me almost every kind of vehicle from bicycles, two- and three-wheeled, to trucks; but a two-wheeled horse-drawn cart brought an involuntary and inelegant exclamation from me at the load it carried:

"I'll bet that's peat."

To my confusion, I heard a masculine and American voice!

"You said it, sister. And that cartload's fuel for the Electric Supply Works, the biggest utilities plant in Ireland. How do you like that?"

70

He was an American soldier; he gave me a kind of salute and a grin as he went ahead of me across the street. I shall never know what he was doing in Athlone, and that annoys me. I speculated about possible reasons as I walked along in the general direction of our *St. Patrick.*

On the bridge I stopped because I saw for the first time, to my right, a lovely, wide and tree-bordered esplanade along the riverbank. Instead of turning left to go down the hill to the boat, I crossed over the width of the bridge, went down a slope and onto the esplanade.

Aware, I think, of the soft haze through which I walked, of the twitter of dry leaves in a light breeze, my mind was as nearly empty as made no matter or perhaps I was half ruminating about that soldier when I realized dreamily an old familiar tune was running through my mind and wondered lazily what in the world had made me think of it. The insistence of the tune and its increasing volume wakened me to a recognition and disbelief that I was hearing an actual band playing in Athlone, Ireland, "Marching Through Georgia." Bewildered, figuratively shaking my head in an effort to clear it, I left the screen of trees and stood on the edge of a broad avenue. I was facing what was obviously a barracks. A complex of stone buildings was immediately ahead of me around a center court withdrawn from the avenue by tall iron gates. These opened as I watched. A military band stepped out, its members vigorously rendering "Marching Through Georgia" with splendid precision. They moved into a packed formation directly in front of me. I moved beyond them. I did not want obstructed my view of whatever was going to happen. Small groups of very young cadets assembled in the courtyard. Officers were stationed at the gates. The groups under orders came into the avenue, wheeled smartly, advanced toward the town and at an order halted. When the full strength of the company was assembled the band advanced to its head, its leader gave the downbeat and they swung into "When Johnny Comes Marching Home Again." By the time I caught up with them they had changed to "The Stars and Stripes Forever." This ended only when the last boy, followed by a now silent band, had gone up the steps and through the doors of the cathedral. The full strength of the company was attending mass.

Lunch was a babel, everyone claiming unique sights encountered, no one listening until the attention of one after another of us was arrested by a kind of chant from Frances.

"Ugliest I've ever seen," she was saying, "positively the very ugliest, and so unnecessarily big. Well, maybe one about fifteen years ago, but not so ugly as this."

Harvey acquiesced enthusiastically. "The only good ones are the old ones, better still, ruins."

Frances gave no acknowledgment of this endorsement. She was in her own world, brooding. "Not even practical," she said darkly.

Harvey seemed unaware he was outside her ken. "That's it," he said. "They're not even functional. Simply bad copies of the old ones, including all the disadvantages that come from lack of knowledge and equipment."

Frances's attention was arrested. The others had resumed their own conversations but I was listening, fascinated and uneasy. There seemed to be two currents of thought here.

Frances was giving Harvey courteous attention. "What did you say, Harvey?" she asked.

"I said, and I'm agreeing with you, that there is not even a practical, as you said, or functional quality about them. Of course, I'm speaking primarily of the interiors."

"The interiors?" Frances echoed. "You mean the insides? I can't say I've ever thought that very important."

Harvey looked at her incredulously. "You mean to say you only look at a church on the outside?"

"A church? What church, Harvey?"

Harvey looked a little wild-eyed, I thought. Frances was smiling benignly.

"What church?" he repeated. "Why, any church. You were saying you never looked inside."

Frances leaned toward him earnestly. "Oh, Harvey, I think you must have misunderstood. When did I say that?"

Harvey, to me, had the appearance of a man sorely tried. He spoke slowly but there was a bite to each syllable. "Just now. You said how ugly the new church was and not even practical and I agreed, and then you said you never looked inside, didn't you?" he insisted.

"I must have been talking aloud to myself. I'm afraid I do that sometimes. It was about a rainhat I bought this morning and I can't think why because it's so ugly and too big to pack easily, and I don't think it's even practical because I believe the rain would drip right down the back of my neck. Of course, I go inside churches. It's the inside of a hat I don't pay attention to."

A sudden and silent appearance of Mr. Kearsley was a fortuitous interruption to what no one could have called a conversation.

Mr. Kearsley was the bearer of unhappy news, he said. He had been talking with the hydraulic power station—powered by peat, I could have told them—and also with the Water Board in Dublin. The representative of each of these monarchs had been sympathetic, regretful and firm. Industry in Ireland must take precedence over the yearning of American tourists to go all the way up the Shannon and there was not enough water for the three of us, the power plant, the Dublin Water Works and the *St. Patrick*. Mr. Kearsley explained further. No one, even among the oldest citizens, could remember in his lifetime such a dry summer as this one had been. "We should be well above water level. Instead we're two feet below. To show you the difference: in winter the river is usually so flooded the callows on either side are so deep the farmers have to evacuate their cattle."

An unfamiliar word is for me more interesting than statistics about water levels. I'm afraid I interrupted to ask the meaning of "callows." Another name for a field, he told me but could not explain its origin.

The men broke in simultaneously. I need not have apologized for my interruption. They wanted to know how the power plant and the Water Works could control the supply and level of the river. There were no unfamiliar words in the explanation and yet I did not understand any part of it. The others may share what was disclosed to them. With no effort on my part I shall keep what I heard a secret. When, in the midst of that scientific gibberish, I heard the words "Supply Board," "eels" and "fish," I came to attention again, not with understanding but with my curiosity aroused. I asked Mr. Kearsley to repeat what he had just said. He obliged.

"The Electricity Supply Board controls the eel-fishing industry and much of the fishing industry. Eeling is big business."

"I never think of the Irish as being eel eaters," Biffy objected.

"They don't eat them," was the answer. "It's all export trade and when the Electricity Supply Board took it over there was—" Not finding words, he shook his head.

"Hell to pay in Jones's Woods?" Sophy suggested. I recognized this as a family expression, a favorite of her father's, though who Jones was and what the particular hell rendered in his woods I never learned.

Mr. Kearsley accepted the suggestion. "That's about it."

Typically it was Biffy who urged him to sit down. She can be counted on to observe the amenities. The idea had not occurred to anyone else. We had only been interested in what he had to say. Mr. Kearsley obliged.

"Well," he continued, "there were families who had been eelers for generations. They grew up to it. They didn't know any other way of earning a living. Suddenly it was taken away from them. I think everybody in Ireland knows about the Hanleys and the O'Haras of Black Island. They were the only families there and they lived off their eeling and fishing. They virtually lived on and from the water, the men and the women, and the children were brought up to it."

He broke off, grinning engagingly. "People said even their cows were water sports and that was no myth. There are a good many small islands, really islets, in that vicinity and the cows swam from one to another wherever there

was fresh pasture. They do to this day. Well, the Electricity Supply Board offered cash token payment that was refused in very certain and colorful terms.

"When the Supply Board bailiffs came face to face with the Hanleys and O'Haras, there was a battle that could have wiped out both sides. It was fog that stopped it. A heavy fog came down between them, so heavy they couldn't tell friend from foe. It routed the bailiffs and in the end the Hanleys and O'Haras too because they couldn't hold out against the might of the whole Electricity Supply Board."

Ellen was indignant and said so.

"A lot of people would agree with you," Mr. Kearsley told her. "And it is a contradictory thing to happen in Ireland because this is a country that looks out for, it protects, the small owner, but in this case the board has swallowed him up. It says it's protecting the fishing and eeling to prevent their extinction by indiscriminate fishing. Their answer is they've been engaged in this for so many generations, by that rule the fish and the eels should be extinct and anybody knows that's not so. Be sure to look at the fish weirs while you're here in Athlone. You'll see a kind of frame for nets but you'll notice there's a gap in the frame. That's a regulation, so that all the fish don't go into the net. A lot of them find and go through the gap. A lot of poachers have found their own gap," he added.

This was the longest time Mr. Kearsley had given us and I wanted more of it. He had already left his chair and still talking was taking gliding steps toward the door. When I asked if he could give me some time during the afternoon, there were things I wanted to ask him, I thought his eyes rolled like those of a startled horse and I know one foot tapped the ground nervously, but he agreed and I pinned him down to a specific time. I knew everyone would have left the boat for further exploring—that is, all but one, Harvey, and he would have to be maneuvered because Mr. Kearsley would bolt at the sight of any audience. Harvey, disgruntled by an unsatisfactory church and the overall aspect of Athlone—"a gray town," one writer called it—would take refuge behind his drawing board. Biffy could cope and she did. She had seen in town, she said, a soft Irish wool throw but she would not buy it without Harvey's approval of the color.

When Mr. Kearsley stood before the chair in which I was reading, the Stevensons were on their way, spiritually hand in hand. The others had gone their separate ways.

Much as I enjoy seeing things, I think I like even better hearing things—music or a story. I wanted to hear about Mr. Kearsley, the *St. Patrick* and how they came together, and he told me. He had been in what he called "hotel business," and I sensed it was an inherited one, in England. Fourteen years before our cruise he had come to Ireland on matters pertaining to his hotel, not a holiday, but he had seen for the first time the Shannon and at first sight known he must live on, by and from it.

"I couldn't explain it to you. It was a bleak time of year and a bleak day but there was something about that stretch of water that came into my blood. I could almost say, but I couldn't tell you why, because I'd never been particularly a water man but there it was. When I went home to England, I told my wife about it, tried to explain to her how I felt and she was a wonderful sport. She said if I could work something out she'd go along. I couldn't get the idea out of my mind. I kept thinking of possible places and I could see them all clearly because after that first sight I'd rented a car and driven up and down, up and down, both sides of the river as close as I could get to it.

"My first thought was a possible combination hotel with the river traffic. I made several trips after that first one and my wife came with me. We looked at hotels and we kept

77

looking at the river. She'd got it as bad as I by that time." He interrupted himself anxiously. "It's hard to explain. I don't know if you would . . ." He looked so embarrassed at this exposure of feelings, I wanted to pat his arm, saying an equivalent of "There, there, it's going to be all right."

Instead I told him brusquely, certainly I understood, would he please go on.

He moved with obvious relief from talking about his feelings. As a practical venture, he said, the Shannon was in the doldrums. Trucks had supplanted river commerce. Barges had disappeared and been put up at auction. That was where and how he had been able to buy the *St. Patrick* and some time after that, the *St. James,* a little smaller than the one we were on.

When I asked who had done the conversion of these boats from freight to very comfortable passenger carriers, he went shy again, clearing his throat, stammering a bit, but finally acknowledging he had done all the designing and had supervised the actual work. Finally, blurting, as if I'd shaken it out of him, he said at one time hoping to be an artist he had studied four and a half years at art school. This admission, of course, explained on the instant his affinity with the Shannon. It was not a practical staid hotel man from England who had driven back and forth along its shores. It was an artist with a fantasy unfolding, of having actually the best of two lives.

With a three-year-old daughter the Kearsleys had moved to Ireland, settling first at Athlone, changing to Killaloe as base because of the water level. I moved rapidly to other questions. I wanted no more talk or explanation of water level. Now, four and a half years after their move, the Kearsleys have four boats and now I knew it was not a tricky, catchy name the Kearsleys had given their business. It is the expression, the visible recognition of the fantasy fulfilled—

the hotel and the river—Irish River Floatels Limited.

There was a nice fulfillment too, a sort of rounding out in the appointment of the captain of the *St. Patrick*. Mr. Kearsley said Anthony not only had been on the river since boyhood but was on the *St. Patrick* when its load, instead of passengers, was barrels that carried sixty tons of Guinness.

"The captain of one of the other floatels is Anthony Donahue's brother. The last two additions to the fleet came from Holland. One of these was a Rhine barge with accommodations for the barge man's family and, in the conversion of this barge, the family apartment was made the dining salon and the galley, below stairs and separate from the lounge above, unlike the plan of the *St. Patrick*." I did not think to ask why these last two additions to the fleet were not available in Ireland, but I did learn the reason a barge was preferable to any other craft. My guess that it was because of the overall length—in England they are called long boats—would have been wrong. It was their depth, Mr. Kearsley told me, and the reason for this stipulation was that it provided a normal stairway.

"Floatel passengers," he said, "are not the kind of sailors who climb ladders."

He was reluctant to talk about the effect of the "trouble" in Ireland on tourist trade but admitted the British quota had fallen off considerably.

"You can't wonder at that," he conceded. "They're involved, but I wish I could get it to other people that here in the south of Ireland we're untouched."

I could corroborate this because we had talked among ourselves about the curious absence in the local papers of any mention of the critical situation we had been reading about in New York. When I asked Mr. Kearsley why he did not emphasize this in his advertising, he smiled ruefully, shaking his head.

"Not allowed to. Government won't permit any suggestion of division in the country."

When I said emphatically certainly his prices would not scare away travelers he brightened and when he spoke it was with a firm determination quite unlike his previous and usual diffidence.

"I'm not interested in what you Americans call 'super deluxe.' I provide comfortable accommodations. It certainly is not roughing it." I agreed. "Good food and every possible attention, but not the fancy extras that have to be tacked onto the price. My idea is to make this a way to see this country and this beautiful river for anybody who can afford to travel at all."

My hand outstretched, somewhat to his surprise, I shook his.

"That's exactly what I've been saying, or trying to say, in every trip I've taken and told about. Other people talk of glamorous travel, special introductions, extra privileges and provisions. They are fascinating to hear or read, but I like to imagine an unknown Mary, Jane, whoever, reading about a trip like this, saying to her husband or friends, 'Why don't we do that?' "

Though various side trips can be arranged according to taste, such as ours to Birr Castle, the basic itinerary is a set one, always beginning at Killaloe and the ending of a two weeks' cruise is at Carrick-on-Shannon. For passengers joining for only one week, a halfway stop is made. In our case, there had to be a change because of the low water level. Change made it, in my opinion, a more characteristically Irish schedule, but I did not share my opinion with Mr. Kearsley. When, however, I commended the organization on the boat and the firmly established itinerary, he smiled with some embarrassment.

"I'm planning to change it," he said. "I've an idea I'm

working on. On a two weeks' trip I'd like to combine one week on the river and a week on land either by car or by horse-drawn caravan, the gypsy type. It would be one week we take care of you and the next you do it yourself and we pick you up. I think this would appeal to certain kinds of travelers. Take the fishermen, for instance. They could stop wherever they liked and for as long as they wanted and certainly the fishing is grand." He had made some Irish vocabulary his own.

"There are times in the season," he continued, "when you can scarcely see the banks for the fishermen, side by side, each under an umbrella and not a word exchanged." When I asked the dates of the season he thought I was referring to the floatels.

"We begin the last Thursday in April to catch the weekend, and go through the first week in October. Of course, for you we extended it another week because you wanted it that way."

Without my asking what had been or were difficulties, he was telling me the hardest thing about running the cruises was getting fresh vegetables and fruit. For the most part, he said, these were not stocked in markets. People grew their own. Also, he added, good meat was not easily come by. The tendency was to export the best quality and what they kept was generally not hung long enough.

"When Mrs. Garrison finds prunes," I told him, "for herself and Mr. Garrison, and I'm sure she will find them, there's nothing more we'll ask for. We've all said how good the food is. I think we do miss greens. Americans are like rabbits about lettuce but we didn't come over here to duplicate what we have at home."

If I had given a cue for her entrance, the timing could not have been more accurate. We heard Ellen's voice outside, calling to someone:

81

"My dear, I've found prunes."

When she came on board, Mr. Kearsley was not there. I had looked away for a moment in her direction.

Within a few minutes after Ellen's return, the roll call, had there been one, was complete. No scheduled meal had brought them back but Maeve must have been watching and counting because a few minutes after the last one was aboard, she brought tea and teacakes just out of the oven. The only even far-off approach to a schedule of meals had been her request to tell her "about when" we would like lunch and dinner served, and Mr. Kearsley's suggestion on the first day that we should not come up too early for breakfast. I think each of us had sensed that to ask for a specific "too early" would make him uncomfortable, so no one had asked. What we had learned for ourselves was that though our nocturnal and matutinal habits were not common knowledge, each one of us turned out to be a "too early" riser, so we had taken before-breakfast walks and then eaten the kind of hearty breakfast we had denied ourselves for years.

While we were having tea and contentedly munching sweet teacakes we would not have touched at home, Ellen asked if she might be allowed to read to us some of the things she had found about Athlone.

We graciously gave her permission and settled ourselves comfortably. She read from L. T. C. Rolt's *Green and Silver* —a book I had on my list to read after I came home from the trip:

"Athlone has been rightly named the key to Connaught. The fortress which still commands the bridge on the Connaught side of the town is a formidable reminder of the importance that was once attached to the possession of this key."

At the moment I could not interrupt her because I did not know it at the time but I can interpolate now that, according

82

to Fodor's *Ireland*, the name Athlone comes from the Gaelic Ath Luain, the Ford of Luan or Luan's Ford. Luan was an innkeeper whose establishment was directly beside this crossing or ford.

Ellen read, "The most famous and the last battle at Athlone was the Battle of the Bridge in 1691 when the Irish on the Connaught side faced the army of William III on the Westmeath bank." (I know now that one Jodert de Ginkell who was William III's Dutch commander at this battle was rewarded for a victory over the Irish by having created for and presented to him the Earldom of Athlone.

Quite apart from the other benefits of this reward, I consider the change of name fortuitous. I like to think that Frau de Ginkell was happy to be called, instead, the Countess of Athlone.)

Mr. Kearsley was among us. "One of the most popular folk dances you can still see done all over Ireland today is called the Bridge of Athlone," he said. "It's very animated. It takes a lot of breath—and brawn."

Albert broke in. "There's a singer," he said, "—I don't suppose there ever was one more loved all over the world, except maybe Caruso—who made Athlone famous by being born here. That's John McCormack."

"Except," Frances contributed, "that we didn't know he was born here until we saw the bust and plaque to him today."

Albert held to his point. "He may have told a few people."

Lloyd's candidate for honors was as typical of Lloyd as John McCormack of the theater had been of Albert.

"I don't know how much you're interested in T. P. O'Connor," he suggested diffidently, and it was equally characteristic of him that he did not say, "I don't suppose any of you have ever heard of T. P. O'Connor," which might have been true.

"Tay T-a-y Pay P-a-y O'Connor?" Harvey echoed. Biffy

with happy surprise gave him a respectful bow. "Born here?" Harvey expanded, "Great fellow, he was. Hot-headed of course; he was Irish. Brilliant journalist and speaker for the national movement. Follower of Parnell. That was in the Gladstone era."

"He wrote a biography of Disraeli," Lloyd offered.

"There's a plaque on the house in the square where he was born," Mr. Kearsley said. Our looks from one to another was an admission that not one of us had seen it.

Ellen, I think, felt she had been shoved aside.

"Do any of you know," she inserted quickly, "that Oliver Goldsmith grew up in a village about eight miles from here? Wait a minute." Forestalling any admissions of knowledge or ignorance, she opened a guidebook at a marked place. The book was *Ireland for Everyman* by H. A. Piehler. That was on my list too. She read, " 'Oliver Goldsmith, the second son of the parson ("the village preacher," "passing rich on forty pounds a year"), spent his boyhood' there. The name of the village is Lissoy and that is the 'sweet Auburn' of 'The Deserted Village.' I don't suppose we could go there?" she added wistfully.

"I don't think you'd find it rewarding," Mr. Kearsley said. "There's really nothing very distinctive about it today. In the poem it's better. Other passengers on this cruise have been keen about the boating here. This is one of the greatest centers for boatbuilding and racing every kind of pleasure boats. They've got their own sailing club and rowing club and they compete all over Ireland. They're very hospitable to visitors who like the sport."

I was frozen with apprehension.

"But I didn't think this would be so interesting for you."

I blessed him silently but with fervor.

"So I got in touch with Mr. English. He's the president of the local museum that is part of the old fortress. He's coming round after dinner to show you over the museum. He's very pleased about this and then he thought perhaps you'd like to visit a pub."

My sigh of relief might, I think, have filled the sail of one of the smaller sailboats. There was general happy agreement that Ellen's voice, raised in anxiety, cut through.

"How lovely. We mustn't keep him waiting. What time is he coming?"

Mr. Kearsley seemed pleased but troubled. "I'm glad you like the idea," he said and almost simultaneously, "He'll come any time you like. After dinner?"

The General was looking at her watch. "I'd no idea it was so late," she said, frowning. "We've got to step on it to change and not stint on our drinks, have dinner and be ready for Mr. English."

Mr. Kearsley was not among us. His voice floated back from the outer passageway.

"Time enough. Time enough."

# 7

Honesty is a virtue I admire and endeavor to express. I resent the sly nudges I have frequently suffered, that I exaggerate. Our visit to the Athlone Museum was an expedition I cannot emphasize, partly because its contents were no great shakes but especially and honestly because the visit to the pub was the more memorable and had the added quality of tending to wipe out everything solely cultural that had preceded it. Mr. English, our guide and friend for the evening, was the president of the museum and pleased to show it to us. The collection had been assembled from local sources by voluntary contributions. Quite apart from the interest of the objects themselves, we told him, was the evidence they gave of the interest he had roused in the community, particularly the outlying farmlands, that would persuade a man working his land not only to take note of objects he might uncover but to take the time and trouble to find out their possible worth and submit them to specialists with the possibility of their being placed in the museum.

There were stone fragments, very possibly Druidical, there were farming and cooking implements and fighting tools. The museum itself was on the second floor of the one-time fortress. It was a wonderful old building, dark with age on the outside, and dark too within from the paucity of windows. Until recently, Mr. English told us, it had housed some of the military but the last of these were now being transferred to the barracks from which I had seen young cadets going to mass. There was considerable discussion, he said, about the ultimate use of the building. Feelings were running high, he added, unnecessarily, I thought. He hoped to keep the museum there as long as possible because interest in the old fortress attracted visitors who might not otherwise seek out the museum. His own involvement came from almost a lifelong interest in archeology. As a boy he had had a curiosity about older civilizations and their way of living, piqued, he said, by objects he himself had found. He was an assayer by profession. From his answers to my questions, I had the impression the term meant both an assessment of land values and their sale at which he officiated as auctioneer. I may be mistaken in this. I have looked up the term and find no mention of its association with anything other than assaying. Mr. English described it with some reluctance that I did not understand, modesty perhaps or possibly snobbishness, a museum head being a cut above an assayer. I accepted his reluctance and so I do not know exactly the business of an assayer in Ireland.

The moment of departure would be, I felt, a difficult one to set. Weighing his kindness in bringing us and his pride in the collection with our eagerness to visit a pub, we must reach and hold a delicate balance. Someday I hope I will learn to cease fretting and leave everything to the General. While I was rehearsing in my mind how to say, reluctantly, "I wish we could stay longer, I'm sure, a mere pub will not

87

have so much to offer"—or "if *only* we hadn't said we would go to a pub"—Sophy spoke.

"It's time we were getting on to the pub. Aren't you getting thirsty, Mr. English?"

Mr. English beamed. "I am that," he said. "The pub I suggest is just a step or two from here. Shall I lead the way?"

Reluctance was not noticeable at the pub. The gale of sound that very nearly blew us backward as the door was opened reminded me on the instant of an inspired suggestion my dearly loved sister-in-law used to toss at a moment of joy: "Let's throw abandon to the winds."

We wedged ourselves on a bench behind a long bare table. We were near the door and might have been on the first row in the theater. All the action was in front of us. There were girls and women, boys and men, all ages and sizes, at smaller tables along the length of the room, just as many, perhaps more, standing two and three deep at the bar. As some of these at the far end shifted position, I looked and looked again at two people who were talking to each other and then to the people around them. That is, they gave the appearance of people talking. In that roaring avalanche of voices I could scarcely get my own to Sophy, who was one away from me, Mr. English between, though my dearest friends and critics tell me I have a carrying voice.

"Look at the far end of the room," I bawled. "Isn't that Frances and Albert?" From her wide-open eyes and mouth I knew she had recognized them. Evidently like me wanting confirmation, she tapped her neighbor and pointed. This was repeated the length of the bench.

We could not believe the two people we saw at an open telephone in, of all places, a pub. It was impossible for us to hear one another. How could we believe Frances and Albert were sending and receiving messages through this *tohu-bohu?* Frances is quite deaf. She is endearingly candid about telling you so, Albert only a little less; he is equally explicit about this. If the angel Gabriel had sounded his trumpet through that telephone I doubt that I would have heard it.

Mr. English leaned close to my ear. "Are those people at the telephone members of your party? Shall I fetch them?"

I squirmed ungracefully from the bench to allow him passageway and took his place. What with the difficulty of making myself heard, and their disbelief at what they thought I was saying, I was making small headway with my companions when our drinks arrived.

Perhaps under calmer surroundings and circumstances, my response to my first sip of Guinness's ale would not have been quite so rapturous. True, my throat was dry from my vocal efforts but my palate had not been strained. I will make no further attempt to justify the immediate rapport between Guinness and me. I will instead acknowledge my anger that I had spent this length of time in Ireland without having tasted it, and my instant realization that if I drank it from now on as I would like to I would gain fifty pounds.

Mr. English returned with the Hacketts. They were happy to see us, happier to be offered drinks.

"Brandy, I think," Frances decided. "It will be more helpful." Irish whiskey was Albert's selection. "I've been drinking beer so there's nothing to fear." For the benefit of Mr. English, who looked somewhat bewildered, Albert recited, "Beer on whiskey, very risky. Whiskey on beer, nothing to fear. It's an American motto," he explained. I reminded him of that next morning.

Frances and Albert sat across the table facing us. They explained alternately, and because years in the theatre had taught them how to project a whisper to the top gallery, we heard every word.

"We didn't go with you this evening because we thought we must telephone London. We couldn't find Kearsley but we met Tony." She looked directly at Mr. English. "He's our captain." Frances's beautiful manners never lag. "He offered to take us to a telephone and this is where he brought us. It was very kind of him but the call has been difficult to make though everyone here has been most helpful. I don't think I've ever been so hot as at that telephone," she added.

Albert continued the explanation.

Singling out Mr. English—his punctiliousness matches Frances's—he continued, "We want Elisabeth Bergner to do a play of ours. That is, it isn't exactly ours, it's an adaptation. I don't want you to think it's an original."

Mr. English had not had an opportunity to be misled, since he had not thought they were playwrights, not thought about them at all until they had been pointed out to him.

"We reached her," Albert concluded, adding, "but I'm not sure we got the message through to her."

A postscript here, I think, is not out of place. Miss Bergner telephoned to the Hacketts' agent in New York a message of bewildered distress. This, relayed to the Hacketts on the *St. Patrick*, bore almost no resemblance to the words they had transmitted from the pub. Weighing the involvements of another telephone call against the cost of transportation, they settled for transportation. Leaving the *St. Patrick*, at the end of our cruise, they flew to London. Since their flight had been booked from Shannon to New York, they had to buy new tickets. After spending a great part of the summer abroad they had allowed themselves to run low on travelers' checks. Sophy, complacently recognized by her friends as the First National Bank because she always carries "in case" more money than all the rest of us, pressed some of it on them to Frances's anguish and Albert's relief. On their return to New York, and the return to Sophy of the money, they reported Miss Bergner could not accept the role because of other commitments. She would have told them that over the telephone had she understood what they were asking her.

"Back at the pub." We realized suddenly and uncomfortably we were bellowing at one another over the shouting and the tumult and there was no shouting nor tumult, only silence and everyone at other tables and around the bar looking toward us politely. Since the age of sixteen I think I've not felt my cheeks so hot. From the color on the faces of my companions I think they were suffering the same experience. We looked at Mr. English.

"Somebody's going to sing, I think," he said, "and generally everybody listens but they didn't want to disturb you." In my opinion, our over-emphatic rush of apologies only made us seem the more loutish and I was thankful when the last of them trailed away.

A young man halfway down the bar waved to us charitably and began to sing. There are carpers, I know, and I do know some, who shudder delicately at the very mention of certain types of singers. Then hear this, carpers and flouters. The day E. Kimbrough does not melt in her bones and innards at the sound of a gondolier in Venice or an Irish tenor in a pub, she will be an old crone mumbling in a chimney corner and I am not there yet. Call it corn or cornmeal mush and be damned. Our tenor was young, handsome, with light brown hair as curly as a poodle's coat and eyes of shocking blue. He sang "A Foggy, Foggy Dew." At its end before the applause and stamping surrounded him, deep sighs were audible all up and down the room. He could not be persuaded to sing again. He finished his drink, I saw the money for it on the bar beside his glass, and went out, turning back at the door to wave and call, "God bless everyone here."

The general talk resumed, almost immediately swelled to a thunderous volume with, like the sounds in a storm, occasional lightning crackle of high-pitched voices.

We were wary of joining the hubbub, we did not want to be caught out again by silence. When another silence did come, as suddenly as if a hand had been clapped simultane-

ously over every mouth, we had not seen what provoked it. Our looks to one another of surprise acknowledged this. The singer, at a table with three companions, was facing us. I had looked at him from time to time, my attention caught by his deep-set eyes under heavy brows and an expression of melancholy conspicuously out of place in these surroundings. I did not see the slightest indication on his part that he was going to sing. He did not leave his seat. He only leaned against the back of his chair with his head high and tilted. His voice was a full baritone and his selection a ballad. Mr. English told me later it was called "The Wild Colonial Boy." Very much later at home in New York I came upon it.

> A bullet pierced his proud young heart from the pistol of
>    Fitzroy.
> And that is how he captured him, the wild Colonial boy.

The singer followed this with another lament. These were received with respectful acclaim. The singer acknowledged it by staring morosely into his glass of stout and shaking his head at the cries of "More." Again by some mysterious signal, the chorus was silent on an instant. We heard a solo voice *speaking*, and heard, disbelieving, the words he said.

> Up from the meadows rich with corn,
> Clear in the cool September morn,
>
> The clustered spires of Frederick stand
> Green-walled by the hills of Maryland.

"The hills of what did he say?" I think it was Lloyd who asked in a whisper and at the same time Frances was mouthing at us, and pointing toward the soloist, "It's our captain. It's Tony. He brought us here to the telephone."

Hissing our incredulity to one another, we must have sounded like leaking radiators. The speaker interrupted his narrative to make an announcement.

"This is in honor of our American visitors," he said and gave a tipsy bow in our direction. "The name of this great poem is 'Barbara Frietchie' and the name of the poet is John Greenleaf [he had a little difficulty with that name] Whittier. And with your gracious permission [another slanting bow], I will begin this fine poem again."

Without his own or anyone's interruption, and without hesitation for a word or proper couplet sequence, he recited the entire poem. At its conclusion, the applause, shouting and stamping were magnificent, and ours was no mean contribution to it. Under its cover Albert made himself heard but only by our table.

"I hadn't remembered that poem was so long," he said.

The proprietor, introducing himself, placed in front of each of us a beaker of Guinness, "Compliments of the house." This provoked a round of applause from the onlookers and a standing acknowledgment on our part.

Albert made himself heard again. "Oh my, I'm back to beer on whiskey. Will that be very risky? Maybe not in Ireland." He was obviously reassuring himself.

Someone gave the cue for silence again. Into it came a voice shaping each word carefully. "Up from the meadows rich with corn,/ Clear in the cool September morn." Two rounds of Guinness later, we tiptoed out of the pub. Behind us as the door closed, we heard Anthony on his fourth go-around from beginning to end, "Up from the meadows rich with corn,/ Clear in the cool September morn."

# 8

"Beer on whiskey is very risky in Ireland," Albert said at breakfast to no one in particular; but to Maeve he said, "Would you make my Sanka double strength? I really shouldn't have that." He seemed to feel the need of explanation and added, "It's not that it wouldn't be good for me. It's that our supply, I'm afraid, is running low?"

Maeve nodded. "It is," she told him.

Albert shook his head regretfully, making little clucking noises. "You see, the doctor has absolutely forbidden Frances to have coffee and I really shouldn't drink it either, but perhaps I'd better have it this morning and keep the Sanka for Frances."

"Take the Sanka now," Maeve encouraged him. "I'll surely find some Sanka in the shops before your supply runs out. It might well have another name, but that won't matter, will it now, so long as it's coffee that isn't coffee?" She did not wait for an answer.

Asking Albert about Frances, I realized his reflexes were a little slow. He was so long in answering I might have thought he had mislaid her.

"Oh yes," he told me finally, "she'll be up later, I think."

He was quicker when I invited him to sit at the table I was occupying.

"No thank you," he said, "I can see you're eating. I think I'll sit over there by myself."

To a slightly, very slightly less degree, the rest of us were subdued. Talk was desultory. Each shied away from companionship. Lloyd told Maeve he would forgo prunes that morning. He confided to me he had also forgone his morning exercises, adding he would just as soon I did not mention this to Ellen. Ellen, coming upstairs at almost that moment, passed us to tell Maeve at the kitchen door she thought she would not want prunes that morning. Returning to the table she searched for her napkin ring—the napkins were always set down haphazardly and we liked that indiscriminate and flexible seating arrangement. Leaning over me to examine the one on my far side, she confided she had not done her exercises that morning. "Only because I was afraid I'd be late for breakfast. I seemed to be taking more time than usual getting up." I nodded, I hoped understandingly, and did not point out that there had never been a fixed hour for breakfast. Lloyd heard her and from his sudden happy smile was evidently reassured. "I didn't do my exercises either," he told her, "nor eat prunes."

Ellen looked at him reproachfully.

"Oh Lloyd," she said, "that was very naughty of you."

The General came in briskly from the outer deck. At the doorway she called, with, it seemed to me, unnecessary loudness, "Good morning, everybody. I've had a lovely walk but I didn't meet a soul. Where was everybody?"

"Biffy has a cold," Harvey said, "and I didn't want to leave her." I shall never again, I am sure, see such a look of utter astonishment as on Biffy's face at that announcement. Harvey rose hastily from the table muttering something about

96

wanting to get things ready for work. He went to the door of the kitchen asking Maeve for two glasses of water and stayed some time making conversation with her, after she had brought him the glasses.

Ellen rarely accepts as complete something that is told her. She wants to be told more.

"When did you get your cold, Winnie?" Ellen is the only one of her friends I have heard call Biffy, Winnie. "I do hope you are taking care of it."

Biffy's reply was terse. "It's not my cold. It's Harvey's and I'll take care of him."

The General, sensing, I think, her heartiness was not well received, joined the rest of us in a silent breakfast.

The silence was interrupted by shrill whistling of boisterous trills and cascades. It may be that all sounds that morning seemed to me overloud. Anthony, the whistler, looked in an open window.

"Good morning to you all," he said. I thought he roared. "We'll be easing away in a little time. I've been to Sean's pub for a little morning jar." A *mot juste*, I thought, if I ever heard one. "He sends you his regards. He hopes you enjoyed his hospitality last evening."

Albert broke in on the chorus of assurances of our enjoyment. "I'm very anxious to get going, Captain," he said. "I'm so keen to see Lough Ree."

Since Albert had made no previous mention of Lough Ree, let alone his impatience to see it, we were all, I think, looking at him surprised.

"In a little time now," Anthony assured him. "It won't be so long, I'm thinking," and resuming his whistling went on his way.

Albert turned to us apologetically. "I was afraid he might start on 'Barbara Frietchie' again," he explained.

We did "ease away" a little after ten, the General pointing

97

out she had shortened her before-breakfast walk because she'd been told by Mr. Kearsley that departure would be at "an easy nine o'clock, or thereabouts."

Lloyd patted her shoulder. "Time enough," he told her, "you'll learn."

Hugh Malet, in his book *In the Wake of the Gods*, says, "Imagine a view of the open sea stretching away to the far horizon but broken occasionally by rounded coasts and archipelagos, and you have some conception of the size of Lough Ree." Its actual dimensions, as I learned later, are eighteen miles in length and at its widest point seven miles in breadth. I also learned that because the countryside is flat, there is no shelter from the wind so that the lough was more often rough than still. It was still for us that day, so still it was hard to believe the landscape around us was not a mirage, its unreality heightened by haze. Polka-dot islands looked as if they were suspended over the water. These were the lush islands, we'd been told, among which cattle, turned aquatic, swam for fresh pasture. The most eerie sight was of a pair of swans motionless in space. There was stillness in the air too. We saw no other boats and our own made so little sound as to be indiscernible from the rustle, like taffeta, of the reeds along the bank. Once in a while a curlew piped sadly and briefly. I do not remember that any of us sitting on the deck spoke.

The sound of Maeve's high heels tapping quickly through the lounge was startling.

"Coming into Lanesborough," she told us as she reached the deck. "And a very lucky crossing too," she added. "This is a treacherous lake."

Mr. Kearsley's announcement wakened us to full attention. He spoke from the near shore and even Harvey left his studio to hear what news he brought. Once in the beginning of the trip, after some prodding by my friends,

98

I had asked Mr. Kearsley when and how he had left the boat to reappear on shore, but this seemed to embarrass him so I never asked again. Now we accepted his appearances as an instance of "Now you see him and now you don't." And there he was on the bank though we had not yet docked. He was embarrassed and apologetic, even distressed, lacing and unlacing his fingers in clasped hands.

We could not go farther on the Shannon was the news he brought. The water level would not accommodate the *St. Patrick*. He was making arrangements for us to go by bus and smaller boats to places that were accessible, but if we wished to cancel the remainder of the cruise, he would return us to Killaloe by car and refund us for the remainder of the trip that had not been fulfilled. I was so preoccupied by an anxiety that by the latest twisting he would never extricate his fingers from that interlocking, how would he accommodate himself to such restriction, that I had not paid attention to the last of his announcement. I came to, startled by the spontaneous uproar that broke out all around me. The phrasing was individual but the sentiment was unanimous: We would not consider for a moment abandoning the cruise. We very much appreciated his making arrangements for us to see other places. We would return to Killaloe by way of the far side of the Shannon and if we repeated one or two stops, we would enjoy their familiarity. I had not intended mine to be a solo of endorsement but I had not wanted either to be the only one who had not spoken. When I had finished, the General was looking at me with a kind of weary detachment. I realized the others were looking at me too.

"That's just what we've all been saying," the General observed. "Where were you?"

After lunch, and what time that was no one bothered to notice, we went our separate ways up into the town. We were docked below what seemed to be an unusually high bridge but perhaps that was because we were anchored below it. Certainly it was broad—the highway ran across it. I counted nine arches that made up its length. For us, the approach to the bridge, the road and the town, was a long flight of very steep stairs. My visual memory is not always sharp. I retain sounds more clearly, but there is no sound so sharp in my memory as the visual imprint of that flight of stairs, the long bridge, a telephone booth at the far end of it and rain pouring down; but all that came later with much between.

Lanesborough is a tidy town, its main street broad and as clean as the sidewalks and the shops and small houses that border them. A dirt side road looked inviting and I followed it downhill around a curve, passing between small houses. Each house had a neat garden in front and each garden was ablaze with dahlias, the largest I think I have ever seen and yet on such strong stems they stood upright and tall, flaunting their bold colors. On my way back to the highway, I think I paused at every garden, seeing other blooms besides the flamboyant dahlias. In a garden near the end of the row some low-growing flowers like rock-garden plants caught my attention because although they were so exquisite in color they held their own against the bright pennants above them. I squatted awkwardly on my haunches to see them more closely. When I got awkwardly to my feet again, I saw a woman watching me from the doorway of the house. I think it was my embarrassment at her having seen me lurching and groaning down and up again that made me feel as guilty as if I'd been caught with my hands full of stolen flowers.

"What a lovely garden you have," I told her. "I was just wondering what the name of these little ones is."

In the first place I am no gardener. Ellen and the General are active and knowledgeable ones. Probably Biffy is too, though I associate her with bird watching. Frances would come next, though Albert would almost qualify with Ellen and Sophy. I am at the bottom of the list. It might seem odd to the lady that I should have to assume a crouching position in order to "wonder." If the lady thought this an oddity she did not show it. Coming down the front walk to join me, she answered with smiling generosity:

"If himself was here, he could tell you now. He's a wonderful man for names, but he's away this verra minute."

"When will he be back?" I asked, hoping to be well away myself by then.

"He will for sure be back in time," was her answer. To change the subject and to avoid going deeper into an Irish timetable, I told her I was on a two weeks' cruise with friends, that we had boarded the *St. Patrick* at Killaloe, named the places at which we had stopped and said we had tied up today just beside the bridge. At this point of my chronicle I realized I was justifying an accusation by my daughters that whenever I make the simplest request of a stranger I include my own and their life histories. I veered.

"Lanesborough is a very pretty town," I told her and she smiled appreciatively, "but the name sounds more English than Irish. Do you know what it comes from?" There I was back at names again.

"Himself could tell you that too," she promised, "and he would have liked the telling of it too." She shook her head regretfully. "But," she added, brightening, "there's something I can show you and it's himself that's made it. If you'll just step up to the door." When we had reached it she pointed up to the lintel.

"There it is," she said, "the name of this house and the town, all in Gaelic, and all carved by himself."

It was a beautiful piece of carving, the characters with scrolls and flourishes around them as delicate as if they had

101

been done in needlepoint. This was the only time during the cruise, indeed I never let it happen again, I had come away from the boat without a scrap of paper. It had been a joy to be able to leave on the boat with confidence my leaden handbag and I had put into my coat pocket only a small wallet that included a pencil through a loop once attached to a memorandum pad. I did find in the other coat pocket a case of matches. There was not space on the inside of the lid for the name of the little house and I will always regret that, but I did write down BEAL ATHA LIAG that is the Gaelic form of Lanesborough, and it means, my hostess told me, a river crossing.

Remembering the potency of the tea I'd been given by another hostess, the one in Athlone, and its effect on my digestion, I declined the same invitation here. My friends would be wanting their tea on the boat, I told her, and would not like it at all without me. How they would have hooted at such an idea, but Mrs. Connery, telling me her name, accepted it. She gave me also the names of two nephews and a niece, living separately in Boston, Gary, Indiana, and Carbondale, Illinois, and I assured her I would undoubtedly run across each of them. I promised to drop by the next time I came round to Lanesborough. "Himself would surely be in by then." We shook hands.

At the corner of the road I turned back. She was at the gate and we waved to each other.

On the main street again, I walked more briskly but I stopped in front of a shop to read with enjoyment the list painted on the window of wildly assorted merchandise to be found inside. When I came to teas and coffee, following glassware, paraffin and petrol, I stopped reading and went inside. I may not have had second sight but I had had an inspiration. In the near corner of the room, his back to the window on which the merchandise was listed, a ruddy-faced man sat at a rolltop desk. His hair was sandy, had once been red, thick, flecked with white, curly and standing up; no brush could have flattened it. He was heavy-set and tall, I could see, because he was leaning back full length in a swivel chair with his feet on the desk. His eyes were half closed. He was smoking a pipe. Reluctant to disturb this peaceful man, I hesitated to speak but he must have heard the sound of the door opening because he opened one eye, turning his head toward me.

"And can you tell me what you would like?" His voice was deep and warm.

"Do you carry," was my answer, "Sanka? It's a decaffeinated coffee, so perhaps you would have it under another name."

In my life I have never seen such a transformation. In one movement his feet were off the desk, his pipe was on it, his arms were above his head, fists closed, and he was shaking them. The voice hurled at me was a roar.

"I do not carry that, and if I did I would throw the slop out of the window! Coffee, by Jesus, is what I carry, not some decaffa-something swill, and that's an end to it!"

It was indeed as far as I was concerned. Before he had finished, I had backed out the door, but his roaring last words followed me.

That night at cocktails, we were talking about the things we had seen and done in Lanesborough. It was the first time we had been together since our arrival there. Frances explained why she had not come up for breakfast and had asked Albert to bring her a cup of soup for lunch.

"I'm fighting a cold," she said. "It's not bad, but do you think it possible I might have had more to drink last night at that pub than was good for me?" We told her this did happen occasionally, reassured her we had not been in the least aware of it about her. She accepted this but added

103

ruminatively, she thought one should guard against such things. "Particularly if you're coming down with a cold," Lloyd suggested gravely.

The subject was finished for Frances. She turned to Albert. "Tell them," she insisted, "the extraordinary experience we had this afternoon at that shop." I have never known Frances to tell an experience she and Albert have shared. She is always the prompter, Albert the chronicler. He obliged.

"We saw a sign on the window of a shop that had, right in the middle of things these shops carry, teas and coffee and we thought here was our chance to get some Sanka because our supply is running low." Looking away from Albert for a moment, I realized all the rest of us were looking at one another, a curious expression on their faces and probably on mine. Albert had not noticed. He continued, "There was a very nice-looking man sitting, leaning back in a swivel chair at a desk, smoking a pipe. As nice a man as you'd want to see. He asked if he could serve us and we told him we were looking for Sanka or any kind of decaffeinated coffee."

Frances broke in. "He turned into a monster. He shook his fists at us. He cursed us. He said whatever it was we wanted was the devil's brew. Tea or the proper coffee, it was God's own making and not de-anything, were the only things fit for a decent man to drink. I never got out of a place so fast in my life." Frances looked at Albert reproachfully. "You went ahead of me and that's not like you, Hackett. The man was crazy, just plain insane, a lunatic. He should be locked up. I think I'll report it to Mr. Kearsley."

The rest of us looked from one to another. Each of us knew exactly what had happened, because each of us had experienced it and each was inviting another to speak. Biffy eventually said it aloud. "Frances," she said, "I doubt the man was crazy. I think what happened was that every single one of us at some time this afternoon went into that shop

and asked for Sanka for you. I know I did. I thought I'd had such an inspiration." She looked around the group. Each of us nodded.

"Oh, the poor man," Frances said. "He must have thought we were crazy."

# 9

The rains came. Sometime during the night I had wakened, heard against the window the sleep-inducing sound of it and responded by knowing nothing more until I was wakened later than usual by the thumps overhead of Lloyd doing his leg exercises. There were no stragglers to breakfast because no one had taken an early-morning stroll. By the time Lloyd rose from his exercises—double, he explained, because of their omission the day before—everyone else, stepping over him, had reached the breakfast table. At along about the third round of fresh toasted Irish bread, Mr. Kearsley came with it from the kitchen. He had not before made an entrance from there and though we were not particularly surprised we were interested. We were surprised by his explanation. Mary, he told us, Maeve's companion, had been dropped off at Athlone because she lived not far from there and had to get back for the term opening of the secretarial school she attended. He was now doing most of the cooking except the teacakes, he inserted quickly, giving Maeve time to do the chamber work. Mary had been little more than a smiling shadow we met in the downstairs corridor sometimes, and said good night to when she went through the lounge with a load of hot-water bottles for our beds bulging over her arms. The surprise was not that she had gone but that Mr. Kearsley was a cook; he turned out to be a very good one, though Maeve, I think, supervised his work.

Our new cook's preoccupation that morning was with an excursion planned for the day. A minibus had been ordered, he said, to take us to Carrick-on-Shannon, where we would lunch and then go by launch up the Shannon to the Boyle River on an expedition to Lough Key Forest Park. Since it was such a rainy day would we prefer to cancel the plan? It needed no discussion among us for this idea to be flouted. We had expected rain in Ireland, we told him. We had come prepared for it. The absence of it had been an unexpected aspect of the trip. Mr. Kearsley appreciated our point of view and was relieved. John Duggan then, he said, with his minibus would come for us at eleven o'clock "or thereabout." At ten thirty—Sophy verified the time—Harvey, stepping back momentarily from the watercolor he was working on, happened to look out the window beside him that in itself looked out on the dock. He called out loud and excitedly:

"There's a car up there. It's just stopped. It looks like a bus of some sort."

Everyone within sound of his voice, and everyone was, rushed to windows or on deck. There was certainly a bus standing high above us on the side road from the bridge. We hallooed and waved but, getting no sign of life from within the bus, hurled ourselves like football players on the mound of outdoor gear piled high on the bench just inside the door, calling with equal velocity for Mr. Kearsley or Anthony or Maeve—or anybody. Anybody did not answer. We were on

108

a deserted ship. Biffy, I think, was the first one coated and rain-hatted; I know, like a skimming swallow, she led the team up the steep flight of stairs, the rest of us panting after her. From the top she called down:

"Don't hurry. He's gone."

We went back down the steps we had climbed. From the dock we saw Maeve and Mr. Kearsley above, turn from the bridge into the side road. They were carrying bundles and string bags but Mr. Kearsley dropped his as Biffy began to talk to him. He left the bags and, on the run, retraced his path across the bridge. Biffy and Maeve joined us on the dock. Biffy had taken over some of Maeve's packages but Mr. Kearsley had told them to leave his, he'd pick them up on his way back. When they reached us Biffy was saying we had called and called when we saw the bus, but had not been able to rouse anybody. She and Mr. Kearsley had gone into the town for supplies, Maeve explained, "and you'd not be calling Anthony at this hour and the boat in port? Unless you'd be putting your head in the door of a pub where surely he's having his morning jar"

Someone had the wit to point out that only a few feet behind us was the *St. Patrick* with an interior dry and warm and we were not progressing to Carrick-on-Shannon by standing dripping on the dock. We got our rain gear off and hung it to dry in any unoccupied space available; some twenty minutes later Kearsley walked into a tenement peopled by restless occupants who all rushed at him as if he were bringing welfare checks. He was not a happy man. He had the look of one whose patience has been sorely tried.

"That John Duggan," he burst out. "I caught up with him in the town. There he was leaning out his bus talking to a friend. I asked him what he was doing, coming and going like that and my passengers standing waiting in the rain, and what did he tell me?" Mr. Kearsley, compressing his lips, drew a deep breath. "He told me he had come when I told him to but since the people weren't ready he'd gone away again. I said eleven o'clock was the time the bus had been ordered and *he* said, this is exactly what he said," and Mr. Kearsley did smile a little, " 'Ah, well, I hadn't the time on me but 'twas surely thereabouts.' He's on his way back—I hope."

We put on our raincoats again and our boots and our rain bonnets as quickly as possible. We would not keep Mr. Duggan waiting again. This time Mr. Kearsley went with us up the steep flight of stairs to the roadside but moved on to stand in the roadway on the bridge like Sister Ann to see if anyone were coming. Once he called back to us encouragingly, "He said he'd be right along." We walked up and down the side road singly, sometimes in clumps, sometimes joining Mr. Kearsley at his lookout. Almost at the moment the General, having managed to work a raincoat and undersleeves up enough to look at her watch, called, "It's exactly eleven fifteen," Mr. Kearsley shouted, "He's coming!"

When the minibus stopped, we were in a docile line at its door like a London queue. John Duggan opened the door on our side but blocked an entry with his arm across it.

"I've just come to tell ya," he said, "I'll not be taking ya now at this minute. Oh, I'll be back," he went on reassuringly, "but since you weren't ready when I came before, I'll wait myself now to take the kids from school. I'd given the job over to a friend but I've seen him in the town just now, I told him there was no need of him, so I'll be back for you sometime after twelve—or thereabouts."

If there was conversation among us on the way down the stairs and into the boat I do not remember it. Mr. Kearsley was not with us.

"I hope he's gone for a jar," Lloyd offered sympathetically. We congratulated Lloyd on presenting an excellent idea for the rest of us to follow and, our garments hung out once more to dry, we had a jar of sherry.

At twelve fifteen, according to the General's report, we left in the minibus for Carrick-on-Shannon. The weather was not unsettled. It was steady, heavy, determined rain, so there was not much of the countryside we could see, but John Duggan established himself as the host of the party, diverting us with information about the countryside we could not see and the people who lived in it. Frequently he interrupted an anecdote to assure us he held no grudge about our not being ready for him the first time he arrived. "I could very nearly say, 'God bless you' for it because, you see, by your not being ready I did not have to hand over the school job to another fellow, so now I've had two in the one day and get paid for the both of them, and besides I'm not a man to hold a grudge."

The rain stopped as we came into the town of Carrick-on-Shannon. It did not slacken. It went from downpour to dryness and the sun came out, so immediately it was as if with each hand one switch had been turned off and another turned on.

Duggan stopped the car in front of the County Hotel, we read on the sign swinging above the door. Each one of us alighting from the bus was groaning and shrugging back muscles stiff and sore after the long drive and each one, reaching the pavement on legs that threatened to buckle because the step down was so high, stood there looking about with pleasure, the aches forgotten. All up and down the street the lampposts were festooned with hanging baskets of flowers and there were flower boxes at nearly every window. Along the riverbank a few yards from the hotel, small craft waved small pennants of varying colors and designs. The sight had helped but not entirely removed the aches of stiff and sore muscles. What they needed and got was a drink in

112

the bar to which we were led by a smiling charming young woman who was waiting for us at the hotel entrance and was evidently a responsible member of its staff. The bar was everything a bar should be in a "county hotel" in Ireland as I had read about them in Irish fiction and biography and heard about them firsthand from no lesser authorities than —and now I am boasting—James Stephens, Padraic Colum and Oliver St. John Gogarty, each of whom I once knew, none of them well, but I have been determined from the start to bring in mention of them.

The bar was dark, with wood paneling and a smell of beer and smoke laced with whiskey. There were high settles around the walls, tables in front of them and a proper bar at one end of the room.

The comfort had long since left us of the eleven-o'clock sherry we'd taken to offset John Duggan's perfidy, but we were delighted to be reminded of it by the offer of sherry or stout, according to taste. The dining room, too, fulfilled descriptions I had read of that room in a small-town or market-town hotel, totally without charm. Distressingly bright, with no shadowed corners to make for coziness and privacy, the tables seating six or more set in rigidly uncompromising rows; there was no Continental nonsense here. The food was as downright and unadorned as the room itself. The waitresses were friendly and as eager about our eating as if they had been our nannies. Toward the end of the meal Frances almost made literal that relationship. We had begun with a rich vegetable soup, moved on to boiled mutton and boiled potatoes and a large serving of boiled cabbage. When a waitress leaning over Frances presented her with a menu, Frances took it uncertainly.

"It's for the dessert," our nannie explained. "You've a choice there."

There had been offered no selection before and seemingly

this was the only menu card. We would wait our turns for our dessert selection. Frances lives, I maintain, in constant anxiety that she has been inconsiderate, even rude. To hurt someone's feelings is to her as shocking as a physical assault. She was murmuring to the waitress apologetically that she really never did take desserts—I doubt that she had often lunched on boiled mutton and cabbage, for that matter— when she caught sight of an item and burst into a kind of childhood rapture. If she did not actually say, "Oh, goodie, goodie" and clap her hands, she was expressing the equivalent when starry-eyed she looked up.

"Is it true," she asked, "that you have rice pudding? Oh, it would be wonderful to have rice pudding. When I was a little girl," she explained to her but with a generous smile of invitation including the rest of us, "my family spent the summer at a place called Little Compton—that's in Rhode Island. We were a very big houseful with grandparents and uncles and aunts and my brothers and sisters. Sometimes there would be sixteen at the table—and Mary, our cook, and she was Irish, my dear, made a great big bowl of rice pudding for us. I would rather have it than any dessert in the world and I can never find it on any menu, but now I've come to Ireland and there it is on the very first menu I've seen." We were all so deeply moved, we told Frances, we begged her to accept our portions of rice pudding. Of course, she would not hear of such a sacrifice but from the size of the portion Nannie set in front of her she might as well have eaten each one of ours. She tucked away every bit of it, scraping the bottom of the dish for the last delectable grain.

During this feast Albert had not taken his eyes from her. I was watching them both. Shaking his head wonderingly, he soliloquized, "And she won't eat one spoonful of ice cream."

114

Frances, looking up from her dish, caught Albert's eye and smiled at him dreamily. "Do you know," she told him, "on the menu there was also tapioca pudding?" She gave a deep sight of contentment. "But I think I made the right choice."

It was half past two, Sophy said, when we left the hotel. The hostess who had greeted us saw us to the door. We shook hands all around. She directed us to turn to the right and we would be at the dock where our launch was waiting. The walk was short, a loitering five minutes or so, and the launch was waiting. So was its owner and captain, Mr. Andrews, who introduced himself and saw us on board. He was from his accent British, not Irish, and from his accent, too, an educated, cultivated gentleman. His boat was scarcely more than half the size of the *St. Patrick* but very comfortable. On the stern deck, a semicircular cushioned bench attracted some of our group who established themselves there immediately. I chose the inside cabin because I could sit on a couch behind a table, talk notes into my Dictaphone of the passing scene that I could see through the windows on either side and be protected from the breeze and occasional spatters of rain.

This was the passing scene as I told it: "The color of the river shades from gold to a beige with a faint pink tinge and then a stretch of dark green. There are four blue herons on the opposite side standing in the shallows. Now startled by our approach they are taking off awkwardly but what a wing span and how beautiful when they are really airborne, their long legs trailing behind them. Now the channel has become so narrow we almost touch the banks on either side. A little farther on it has widened to half a mile or more across. The sun comes and goes. The light is constantly changing. Now we are between trees whose lowest branches touch the water. I have not seen a house. The landscape is widening to meadows and hills, stone walls marking the fields. We

have just gone under an ivy-covered bridge of three arches. I
wish I had counted the number of bends we have gone
around, perhaps Sophy has. The scene is changing color constantly. Now we are going between woods on either side, thick
beautiful trees, the foliage of some is already changing color.
There is a lock ahead and two other boats in front of ours.
We have gone up the Shannon into the Boyle River and
after this we will be in Lough Key."

The others were halloing to me. I left the cabin and my
note-talking.

When I joined them, our group was alongside the occupants of the boats ahead of us, all sitting along the broad
stone top of the lock channel. Conversation among us was
spontaneous and easy. Each wanted to know the starting
point and the route of the others. Harvey told us the name
of this was the Clarendon Lock and when we praised him

for having done his homework ahead with his map, he admitted with commendable honesty he had gotten the informa-
from Mr. Andrews.

"However," he added, "this is of my own perceiving." He pointed to an inscription in the stone of the wall across from us and we read, "Clarendon Lock, built 1848, under V.R." Here in this remote backwater in Ireland at a lock operated by hand was the stamp of an empire and its ruler, Victoria Regina.

The operator of the lock was a very young man, not yet twenty would be my guess. He had black hair shoulder-length, deep blue eyes and a whiter skin than the ruddy complexions to which we had become accustomed. Talking to him briefly, I felt an overall sadness, a kind of hopelessness about him. When I answered his questions about where we came from, he said he was sure he'd never get to New York, "though it must be, I've heard, the most wonderful place in the world."

When I asked him about the schedule of the locks I was glad Sophy was not within earshot.

"Somewhere around ten I open the lock," he said, "and I close it along about six or eight, but tomorrow, it being Sunday, I'll shut down close to noon." His smile was not a happy one as he added, "We have to go and pray—for peace—and it doesn't do any good at all."

This was the only time on the whole cruise I heard mention of the "trouble" in the North.

Albert and Lloyd helped close the lock gates. Everyone went back to the place he had occupied before as if he had been assigned to that seat and I resumed my notes.

"Now there are meadows on the far side with hills beyond. There are even higher hills ahead. We are in Lough Key and it is dotted with small wooded islands. There's a silver light over everything. It is misty in the distance. A sudden

117

spurt of rain ends as suddenly as it began and over the hills on my left is a perfect rainbow. I shout to the others. Answering cries are, they'd already seen it. If I would come outside I would see a good deal more. I do not answer this but continue my notes. We are passing a large flock or whatever a cluster of swans is called. Now the sun is out again. A castle comes into view. I shout out a request for its name. The answer comes back that Mr. Andrews calls it 'another Victorian folly.' Whatever its name, this is an accurate description. It is a house of a size that justifies calling it a castle and is cramped on so small an island there is scarcely room around it for so much as a lawn. We are slowing down. There are shouts from outside that we have reached the Lough Key Forest Park."

We had just left the launch and were looking about, uncertain which way to start exploring, when the luck of the Irish came our way in the person of Mr. John Duane; he had arrived at the dock on some errand. Seeing our uncertainty he offered his services as a guide. With an instinctive aversion to professional guides we seemed to share, each of us drew back involuntarily. Mr. Duane shyly and modestly introduced himself and his credentials for guiding. He was the Chief Forester of the park.

Perhaps from embarrassment I think we were effusive in our grateful acceptance of his offer but it seemed to thaw his own shyness. The park, he told us, comprises 850 acres and was acquired by the Forest and Wildlife Service from the Rockingham Estate, sold by its last owner, Sir Cecil Stafford. He accompanied this piece of information with a wide sweep of an arm to indicate the magnitude of the property and narrowing the gesture to point ahead of us and to our right, said he would lead the way up the trail.

At that moment I had my first misgivings. An hour later I regretted the Chief Forester had lost his shyness. At the end of two hours I would have been willing to settle for less than the luck of meeting the Chief Forester. Finding a four-leaf clover would have been less of a strain on the legs. Admitting this as I plodded along, I recognized it was churlish and that I would admit it to no one else because actually there was much to see and Mr. Duane, unlike a professional guide, was as enthusiastic as he was informative, obviously loving the place and his job. There were things we might have passed by—reaching a certain fatigue level, I am one for passing by—or would not have understood had we seen them. The ringforts, for example. Five of these are within the park and one of them contains a "souterrain," which makes it the more unusual. The ringfort, we learned, is one of the ancient monuments in Ireland. Their building and use was begun in the second or third century B.C. and continued to the seventeenth century A.D. It is known also by other names—rath, liof, dun or cashel—but Mr Duane did not say how these other names came about, only that it was a kind of fort in the shape of a ring, a strong protective structure built around a farm, providing at the same time a defense and an enclosure for the cattle and sheep. Some of these ringforts contained underground passages, he told us, and chambers that were called "souterrains." These passages were narrow, scarcely large enough for a man to crawl through. They led to small chambers, the souterrains. These were used as cellars, providing storage space for grain, but they undoubtedly were also a place of refuge for the women and children in time of danger. During the eighteenth and nineteenth centuries, he also told us, when large estates were being landscaped, it became fashionable to plant rings of trees. Many times these were set on an existing ringfort, occasionally constructed specifically within a circular bank and ditch. Therefore these tree rings are occasionally mistaken for the older and original ringforts.

119

The forest is magnificent and well deserves having the park named in its honor. Mr. Duane said many of the great trees are of the original plantings at Rockingham. In the eighteenth century among the great estates there was intense rivalry for trees. It was a mark of prosperity and therefore these woodlands were designed for ornament or for prestige, not for the sale of timber. We paused at a grove of bamboo because, Mr. Duane pointed out, though the bamboo is not a tree but really a grass, nevertheless the fact that it had been imported from the Far East brought the owners great prestige and, he added, "considerable envy, I'm sure, because the news of this was widely carried."

We were not at the time of year to see the full blooming in the bog garden but we were very pleased by its design and Ellen and Sophy behaved somewhat like Irish setters, nosing about among the plants, darting in one direction and then another, exchanging sharp cries of discovery. I took a calmer interest in the fact that the garden was superimposed on a peat bed and that the plants chosen were "peat loving." The plan of the garden includes a true maze of pathways, that surround a small wooden bridge. The main pathway is paved with cross-sections of oak trunks cut from the forest, one of the loveliest as well as most unusual paths I have ever seen. Mr. Duane told me these stepping-stones of oak trunks have been sunk more than a foot deep in the soft peat. We were not so interested in the deer enclosure and the recital of the small wild animals to be seen with luck in the park, none of them particularly unusual. Lloyd and Biffy gave a wistful moan or two in response to Mr. Duane's listing of bird life to be seen given time enough to take up a protracted bird watch. We were not so interested in the icehouse preserved from the original estate, as the story that the first refrigerative structure was built in England in 1660 for Charles II. We liked the verse that recorded it:

Yonder, the harvest of cold months laid up
Gives a fresh coolness to the royal cup;
There ice, like crystal firm, and never lost
Tempers hot July with December's frost.

Mr. Duane told me as we were walking through part of the forest a verse I wrote down at his dictation, because of its charm and because it reminded me of a saying my grandfather in Indiana had told me when I was a very little girl. After all the years between, Mr. Duane explained the reason for the saying. The verse reads,

If the oak's before the ash
Then you'll surely get a splash;
But if the ash precedes the oak
Then you may expect a soak.

Grandfather's was a precept followed by farmers:

When the acorn is the size of a squirrel's ear it's time to plant the corn.

Mr. Duane explained the reason the oak was the forecaster of the season was that it and the ash are the last trees to come into leaf. Consequently, I suppose, their evidence was more dependable. Early budders were giddy and impulsive, responding daftly to early sun, though frost might follow. I had not known also, and I owe this bit of information to Mr. Duane, that because the oak was the tree that grew in greatest number in ancient Ireland, supplying for centuries the timber for houses and boats, a corrupt form "derry" of its Gaelic name, *dair,* became the most widely and commonly adopted tag to place-names throughout Ireland, and I immediately thought of "The Londonderry Air."

As we talked I had been gently easing Mr. Duane in the direction of the landing, our boat and the soft couch in it where I had sat. When Ellen joined us my love for her

121

teetered. I knew she was going to lead him afield again. What restored it to firm ground was a realization of my freedom of choice. Let the indefatigable Ellen lead him where her "satiable curtiosity" directed. Let others follow their separate and wayward paths; mine would be a direct one to the boat or to a place to sit down.

When the others came straggling home, I was sitting comfortably on a stone coping at the landing. I was relaxed, rested and enjoying the sight of small boats coming and going across the little harbor in which we were docked. Ellen and Mr. Duane were the last arrivals. He had eagerly answered her siren's call to explain something she had seen and from the expression of discomfort on his face, I think he was regretting it. I gathered what she had asked him to identify was a considerable area that had been marked off, and within it, evidence of some project under way. They stood near me on the landing continuing their conversation—that is, Ellen was continuing; Mr. Duane seemed to be trying at intervals to say goodbye.

"I really do hope," she was saying, "you will seriously consider what I have been urging you. I think it's probably a nice idea," she continued dubiously, "to have that a camping space for caravans, lovely for them, of course, but they really must be tidy, you know, for the sake of the park and other people. And for their sakes you really must not allow too many at a time or they will feel they have come to a tenement."

Mr. Duane murmured, these things had indeed to be taken into consideration, and tried again to say goodbye.

"But you see," Ellen continued "people really don't think of all these things and then it's too late. Your park is so beautiful it would be a great pity to have too many people seeing it all jammed up together because then you see they wouldn't feel they had come into the country at all. And of course you must consider the animals and the birds too. Of course, I'm sure Irish people aren't vandals going around picking flowers and things but after all—"

Mr. Duane said goodbye again.

Lloyd put his arm through Ellen's "The captain, I think," he said, steering her toward the boat, "wants us to come aboard. We must get back to the lock before closing time."

We were at the lock past closing time, but the boy keeper had waited for us.

"There was no special reason to close it," he said, "time enough."

Sophy and Biffy helped close the gates with a conspicuous display of muscular strength in a rather show-off manner, I thought, as I supervised from a distance the operation. Ellen and the men, their backs turned to the workers at the gate, were talking to the people I recognized as I joined them. They had been in one of the two boats ahead of us when we had reached the lock on our way up. They had found the place, Clarendon Lock, so delightful they had decided to tie up there for the night, going on the next morning. Ellen gave them valuable information about what to look for, especially in the park, urging them to write it all down as she talked. Under Lloyd's persuasion, but reluctantly, she left them.

# 10

Frances was at the far end of the cabin from me. I had not realized she was there. I had been absorbed in the passing landscape and talking about it into my machine. The overall light was a shimmering silver, the air was misty, the rain seemed to be holding off reluctantly. Now the reeds were

pale yellow in places and pale green in others and sometimes a deep russet. What I had not been aware of before was that frequently they lined the water's edge as evenly as if they formed a clipped hedge. The overall mistiness seemed to give an added sense of unreality and remoteness, but suddenly we were under a bridge and as we slipped quietly along our channel, immediately overhead a truck thundered past. The sudden roar in that stillness was so unexpected I was jolted and looked wildly around for a moment of alarm that the noise had come from within the boat and I saw Frances. She was sitting behind a table on which she had spread a considerable number of postcards. Evidently she was as startled by the noise as I had been. She jumped involuntarily and immediately turned to rummage in the handbag beside her. As I watched she took from it a compass, looked at it, then again and after the second look shook it violently. In the act of shaking it she noticed me.

"This has never happened before," she said. "My compass has betrayed me. Whatever is the matter with it? It must be stuck. This indicates the same course we followed before."

"That's because, I suppose, we're going back the way we came."

"Oh, I don't think so, dear," she suggested politely. "It looks very different and you remember we went through a lock before."

"I think it's the mist that makes it all look so different." I was polite, too. "And we've just been through that lock."

She was astonished but not argumentative.

"I must have been looking at my postcards," she reasoned. "I got some really lovely ones."

Frances, I am sure, had not covered more of the park than I, and I had not seen so much as a counter, let alone a building in which postcards were stocked. It is rather a shivery thought but I wonder if given the opportunity Frances might pick up a few on the moon.

There was a time when I would have been surprised to see Frances consult a compass, not just any compass but her own. It is not usually included in the basic accessories to a woman's handbag like lipstick and compact, but over years of friendship and travel with Frances and Albert I have seen her take a compass more frequently than a lipstick from her bag. It was a long time ago too when, my curiosity exceeding respect for privacy, I asked how she had happened to include this among her toiletries. I have not forgotten her explanation.

"Oh," she had said, "I bought it because we were looking for a flat in London."

Evidently my response to this explanation had not displayed total enlightenment. She expanded it, her raised eyebrows indicating she had not expected me to be quite so mentally slow.

"Why, my dear, you know how seldom in London one gets a sunny day, so Albert and I wanted to be sure that when one did come along, our apartment would be facing a direction to take advantage of it, and when you've gone into a building of flats, up an elevator, down the corridors, you lose sense of direction, so I bought a compass and I've never been without it since."

Only a few minutes after she had returned to her postcards and I to my notes, we looked up and at each other again simultaneously. The boat was obviously slowing down, in fact, coasting, whatever the nautical term for that is. If we were returning the way we had gone, we could not possibly be reaching by this time Carrick-on-Shannon. Frances, having got her bearings, was aware of that too. Out the window I could see we were about to come alongside a landing. Lloyd stood in the doorway to the stern deck.

"All ashore as is going ashore," he called jovially. "End of the line. We go by car from here."

By the time we had reached the deck, postcards gathered up, the others were ashore. Mr. Andrews and another man were waiting alongside to give us a hand. Mr. Andrews introduced us.

"This is my partner, Mike, and this is our boatworks. We've two cars here. We're going to take you to a famous pub. Your bus will pick you up there."

Mike was tall, blond and deeply tanned. For all that his name was Mike, and I never learned his last one, by looks and speech he was an Englishman, and he was charming. We walked along the road together. The cars, he said, were a bit farther on.

In the middle of our conversation, I stood still and stopped talking. We were the leaders; I think Mr. Andrews had been showing the others the boatworks. I was looking at what might have been a trailer camp but was accommodating instead three or four gaily painted horse-drawn caravans. It was a picturesque sight but what made it the more arresting were the occupants. I have seen gypsy caravans in Greece and in Portugal and have seen their occupants, dirty, shifty-eyed, the children scrawny, sickly and filthy.

There were children playing on lowered steps from the caravan nearest me. They were healthy and scrubbed. Seeing us, they interrupted a game they were playing and called, "Good afternoon." A young woman came to the doorway at the head of the steps. Evidently reassured by the sight of the strangers to whom the children were speaking, she waved to us cordially.

"Having a good holiday?" Mike called.

"Wonderful, wonderful," was her answer. She was wearing a silk shirt, open at the neck, slacks of dark green and around her short curly hair a bright yellow ribbon. Gaping, I took in all of this because I had never seen such gypsies as these, and I said as much to Mike as we walked on. He laughed.

"It's a fad, sprung up all over the country, a new form of camping and a great lark for the kids. They hire a caravan for a week or a fortnight's holiday around a spot where there's good fishing or sailing or maybe a golf club nearby for Mummy and Dad. The kids learn to take care of the horse and they're not cooped up squabbling in the back of a car. Sometimes they run alongside on the road and if the night is fine they sleep outside in a tent or a sleeping bag. But," he continued, "in Ireland you don't talk about gypsies. They're tinkers. You'll find gypsies on the Continent and in England but very few in Ireland. There are some towns —Athlone used to be one of them, I'm not sure whether it still is—that have a tinker colony but for the most part the tinkers are nomads. They will always gather at the big fairs in Ireland. They're like the gypsies in that they're horse dealers and fortune tellers, not much any more of selling and mending pots and pans that the name comes from, of 'tinkering.' "

Later, in my post-trip reading, I found more information about the tinkers from L. T. C. Rolt's book *Green and Silver*. He writes, "They have their own secret language though it seems doubtful whether this tongue is still used in its pure form but only in an admixture of cant, Romani, Gaelic, back-slang or that other secret language of the Masons, the ancient Gaelic of Bearlagair na Saer. One of their chief rallying points in the West is the sheep fair at Ballinasloe, where they elect their king. They have their own code of honor and punishment. One family will help another financially if it is down on its luck, upon pledge that the debt is repaid when the two meet again at a certain fair. Woe betide the debtor if he ventures to appear without being prepared to honor his pledge. Debtor and creditor are involved in a free-for-all in which all the tinkers join with a will. The result is a pitched battle such as took place at Portumna Fàir a few years ago when 'the blood was running in the gutters and that's the truth, I'm telling you.' "

Henry's was the pub to which we were driven. Though we were told it was famous and very old, the exterior of the building that housed it was modern plaster with no adornment. Henry welcomed us to the bar, shaking hands all around, passing to each of us his advertising calling card that was well worth keeping, and asking our orders, saying at the same time it was Guinness we must drink. The heading at the top of the card reads, "Cead mile Failte" and below that in smaller letters "to," then in large capitals, "Henry's" and under that, "Cootehall, Boyle, Co. Roscommon." I think the heading, but I neglected to ask, in Gaelic means something like "a six-mile drive to Henry's" because at the bottom of the card are specifics: "Boyle: 6 Miles, Carrick-on-Shannon: 6 Miles."

According to his card there is more to Henry's than the bar contains. It advertises under "Select Bar and Lounge," "Fishing Tackle and Calor Gas Dealer." "Visit Our Grocery and Hardware Store For All Your Requirements" and below that, "A pleasant evening can be spent at our Lounge Bar." But on the back, or perhaps it is the front of the card, it becomes waggish; it is headed: "Free Pass to Friends." It has in the left-hand column, "You May Wear Many" and opposite is the reproduction of a diamond from a deck of cards. Below this on the left-hand side, "You May Belong To Many" and opposite, the reproduction of a club. Left-handside again below, "You May Have A Big" and opposite it, a red heart. Left-hand side below, "But You Don't Need A" and opposite, a spade. Bottom line, "To Dig Up Our Location (see other side)."

We took our drinks to benches in the corner and invited

129

Mr. Andrews and Mike to join us. The conversation was general until I realized I was overhearing bits and pieces between Lloyd and Mr. Andrews and that there was considerable confusion in them. Answering a question, Mr. Andrews had said he was a graduate of Dartmouth. That prompted Lloyd to express pleasure at the choice and the hope he had enjoyed his years in America.

When I came in, Mr. Andrews was floundering under these sentiments. Apologizing for my interruption, I volunteered the information that I happened to know Dartmouth was the Annapolis of England. That cleared the misunderstanding. I took advantage of the clarification immediately because I like to know about people and asked how he and Mike had come together and come to Ireland.

Mr. Andrews obliged. He had served for twenty-two years in the British Navy, rising to the rank of Lieutenant Commander, and by that time he had had enough and yearned to leave the sea and settle down. He had found Mike to be of the same inclination. They had served together for a long time. He said no more of Mike's background or rank, only that they had the same objective: "messing about in boats." They had traveled widely over the Continent and come to rest in Ireland "because it's unspoiled." They had an opportunity to buy the boatworks at Cootehall and had not regretted it because it not only included boats to hire but a service to other firms of reconditioning their boats over the winter because, he said, "presumably we knew something about boats." They had done very well until recently, "but now the English trade is dead—the English won't come to Ireland." (Just what Mr. Kearsley had said to me.) They were getting instead Germans, Japanese and Americans but most of these did not want either a run-yourself boat or a long cruise. Therefore the partners were selling off their for-hire boats and buying from England or having made there launches that would hold forty to fifty people for day excursions such as the one we had just made. They planned to combine these with coach tours to the Yeats country, "which is becoming a boom objective for tourists, like a pilgrimage." They would then meet the coaches and return the passengers by launch.

He was enthusiastic about this prospect, speaking more quickly than before and a little louder. They would make the launches very comfortable, he elaborated, with every possible attraction including Muzak. I think Mr. Andrews regretted his enthusiasm. It attracted Ellen. She overheard the word Muzak though she was half turned away; but turning quick as a bird in flight she leaned toward him across the table between, her hands clasped earnestly.

"Oh, Mr. Andrews," she said fervently, "I beg of you please do not add that dreadful Muzak. Of course it's not that I think music is dreadful. My husband and I love it very much, concerts and records that we play, especially in the country on weekends and especially when I am in the kitchen because I do think that's very boring, don't you?"

Mr. Andrews nodded dazedly. Ellen, I think, did not notice. She continued:

"But don't you see, music coming from a boat on the river is very different because it would reach other people on boats and be disturbing. I think it would change the whole spirit of the river. I do hope you will consider that."

Mr. Andrews ventured to say faintly, he was under the impression people enjoyed it.

Ellen conceded this dubiously. "Well, possibly, but I would so appreciate it if you would promise to play it very softly."

Mr. Andrews was rescued by Lloyd from either capitulating or holding his ground. Lloyd took Ellen's arm.

"Dear," he said, "the bus has arrived. We must go."

Ellen capitulated only partially, but with charm.

"Goodbye, Mr. Andrews," she said, holding out her hand,

"you've given us a beautiful day on your lovely boat and I'm sure you'll play your music very softly."

We said goodbye to Henry at the bar and came out to blinding rain, the heaviest we had been in during the whole cruise, and a two-hour drive ahead of us.

Although the space in the minibus was cramped each of us sat in miserable isolation. The dampness seeped in, so did cold air. There was fitful conversation and then there was none. We traveled on bumpy dark roads. I am, under the best circumstances, a nervous woman in a car. Even in my misery I had room for apprehension that another car or perhaps a cow would appear in the darkness out of nowhere. When after what had seemed to me about six hours of driving, what did loom up out of the darkness were the lights of the town and the sign LANESBOROUGH. I could have read it "The Promised Land." From the sighs and "thank God's" around me I think my reading was unanimous.

Among the greatest, I count the wonders a hot bath, a change of clothes, a drink and food can perform. We dined at nine. Conversation was animated, spirited and gay. We were nearing the end of the meal when I said an hour ago I would not have thought it possible that at this moment I could scarcely remember the fatigue of the day and the misery of the drive home.

Shaking her head, Sophy made little clucking sounds of sympathy. "I hope you're not forgetting you have to telephone the Jaffes right after dinner."

She might just as well have poured a bucket of rainwater over my head. I could feel it trickling down my spine. Around the table there was a chorus of sounds without words, of sympathy.

"I know," Sophy said, "it's awful but you've got to. This is the night you said you'd call them to make sure they're coming, and to set the place and time for our meeting."

There was a pause. "I'll go with you," she added.

Never before had I known, and I would never again experience, such proof of friendship, I told her, and she agreed.

Back into outdoor clothes and damp raincoats and hats again! To our grateful surprise, Albert, dressed for the weather and carrying an umbrella, joined us. I was more grateful than surprised when out of the mist at the foot of the stairs Mr. Kearsley took shape. It was ten o'clock now and from the top of the stairs across the bridge and into the town we could not see a single lighted shopwindow. The streetlights themselves were widely spaced and, in the rain, flickering and yellow.

At the far end of the bridge a public telephone booth was an island of illumination. Heads down, we plodded to it across the bridge. That is the scene I shall never forget. A telephone booth in spotlight, the focal point of the town, the sound of the rain on its roof as I stood inside, door open, the others in a half-circle behind me; in front of me on the shelf coins of enough variety to make any necessary combination possible, spread out like an arrangement of cards for solitaire. Facing levers and buttons to be operated properly as well as coins, I was baffled. Like figures in a square dance Mr. Kearsley and I changed places. He put in the call and inserted the coins. After a very short delay there was a violent regurgitation. Of the two possible numbers for the Jaffes in my address book, I had chosen the wrong one. This one had been disconnected. I had thought the drive home from Henry's Pub the nadir of misery but it was not. I had thought having to dress again in damp clothes, leave the warmth and comfort of the *St. Patrick* was the nadir of misery but it was not. We really touched the bottom when the coins spewed out at us.

Albert's is the stuff of which saints are made.

"I'll be back in a jiffy," he said and was gone, running to the bridge, his umbrella bouncing about over his head. We watched him for the few yards we could see him and then we waited. I do not remember that we talked but I suppose we must have exchanged a few words. It seemed simultaneously a day and a minute when we heard his steps on the bridge again. We marveled that he could have made the trip in such a short time and told him so. He could only nod a smiling acceptance. He was too out of breath to speak. He brought from an inside pocket and handed to me a slip of paper with a number written. Underneath in Frances's writing was, "I'm sure this is the right one. We used it when we called them in London two weeks ago."

Once more the coins were spread out on the shelf. Mr. Kearsley, taking from me the paper with, we hoped, the magic numbers, entered the booth. Sophy, Albert in the center endeavoring to share his umbrella, and I crowded the doorway. Mr. Kearsley pushed the button, pulled the lever, inserted coins and we waited. The rain on Albert's umbrella and the booth was the only sound until Mr. Kearsley's "Just a moment, if you please," loud and clear into the telephone made us jump. He backed out and I took his place.

"Hello," I said quaveringly, not yet believing it could be true, and back to me came the warm, rich, deep voice of Sam Jaffe in London.

"We're just back from Moscow," he said. "Just walked in the door. If you'd called fifteen minutes earlier you wouldn't have reached us." (It was the hand of the Lord, not mine, that had written down the wrong telephone number. Had I called the right one and got no answer, I would have assumed they had not got back from Russia and so would not join us.) "Give us a day or two to get reorganized. We'd like to make it tomorrow, we want so much to be with you, but how about Monday?" In well under three minutes it

134

was settled. Banagher on Monday, some time in the afternoon. They would hire a car at Dublin Airport and find us tied up at the dock below the bridge at the bottom of a downhill dirt road just off the highway. When we reached the *St. Patrick* for the last time that night we were singing in the rain.

# 11

Next morning at breakfast Albert, giving his order to Maeve, said, "The Madam has a slight cold." He would take some Sanka and toast down to her later. When Maeve had returned to the kitchen, I chided Albert again for his choices of nomenclature.

"First you tell Maeve she's the lady you are traveling with and now you refer to her as the Madam."

Albert was indignant. "It's a term of endearment," he protested.

"It has a very unfortunate connotation," was my answer.

"Very flattering," was Albert's. The others who were there hooted at me derisively.

Biffy always comes to the rescue of anyone who is being derided.

"It's the Indiana in her," she said quickly. "She can't help it. It comes out in her every once in a while. She goes Puritanical."

Ellen does not like bypaths in conversation. They make her uneasy. She likes to hew to the line.

"If Frances has a little cold, Albert," she said, "we must do something about it right away. It's very important to check a cold at the beginning. Now I have some excellent cold medicine. It's—"

Albert raised a protesting hand. "No use, Ellen. She won't take it. She will not take medicine."

"Religion?" Lloyd asked, with interest.

Albert shook his head. "No," he said, "suspicion."

"Then what are you going to do?" Ellen demanded.

Albert considered this. "Try to keep her out of drafts. I think I'll put her in a bell jar."

Ellen is as wary of sallies as Frances is of medicine. Ellen was perplexed. She frowned and returned to her prunes.

The door from the outer deck was butted open by Sophy, who then turned round displaying an armload of newspapers. She was followed by Frances carrying an equal supply.

"Good morning," they said almost in unison and no one answered. They eased their bundles to the book table, dropped their coats on the bench that was our coat closet, came to the breakfast table and Sophy inquired, "Is no one speaking to us? Are we out of favor?"

Ellen addressed Frances. "Albert said you had a cold and," with emphasis, "that you won't take medicine for it. Now I really do think—"

Albert interrupted. He was indignant. "You said last night you thought you might be getting a cold. I don't know how you got out there. I tiptoed so as not to disturb you."

Frances was amused. "I tiptoed out so as not to disturb *you*. You were sleeping so peacefully and it's only a little sniffle anyway." To Ellen, apologetically, "Medicine always seems to work the wrong way with me. Perhaps," appeasing the whole pharmaceutical world, "that's because I distrust it."

Albert was not appeased. "There you were out on the town

and I tiptoeing out of the cabin carrying my clothes. I dressed in the corridor behind my hand."

Sophy amplified. "Frances and I met at the coat bench. She wanted a breath of fresh air and I suggested we find newspapers."

Frances interposed, "So that we would know it's Sunday. They do go together."

We heaped praise on them and rushed for the newspapers, leaving Frances and Sophy to have their breakfast. After that there was the universal contentment a Sunday morning with newpapers brings. When Maeve ran through the room to the deck, we knew we were leaving Lanesborough. The General looked at her watch. "Eleven thirty," she said. Harvey, putting down his paper, grinned. "Time enough," he said. "I think I'll do a little painting," and moved to his workshop table.

He did not stay long. He did not even start to paint. On the way from the kitchen the jars of water he was carrying sloshed over and he slued a bit himself. We were into Lough Ree and headwinds. Biffy, Lloyd and Sophy went on deck and I joined them. The sky was overcast; there was no rain but we were very soon drenched by spray. We were not in fog, but a heavy mist. Lloyd pointed out how difficult it must be to follow the channel because the buoys that indicated it, red for port side and green for starboard, were poorly marked at best and in atmosphere such as this scarcely distinguishable. He added Anthony could probably steer the course without any buoys at all.

No birds sang or flew, so, chilled, damp and unable to keep our footing or hold down a deck chair, we came indoors. Ellen in her own corner of the couch was barricaded by a wall of books. The Hacketts across from each other, the table between, were selecting from their collection and writing postcards. Harvey was restless. Deprived of his painting and finished with the newspapers, he said he wanted conversation. He suggested I tell him about the Jaffes since he and Biffy were the only ones who didn't know them. Sophy urged me not to "oversell" them.

"It's the Midwest coming out in her," she explained. "You know, she's a 'booster.'" It was the second time that morning my Middlewestern roots had been brought to the surface, and far from resenting it, I gloried in it, but I conceded Sophy's point.

"It's like someone introducing two people and saying, 'I know you're going to love each other.' At that instant they hate each other."

Harvey amplified. "Or like your mother when you were a child, expecting you to take to another child because the mothers were friends. The result? Intense dislike, if not bloodshed, each time they met."

I promised to undersell the Jaffes.

"To start with, I adore them," I began and at Harvey's quizzical look, "All right, I'll begin again. We met sometime during the forties in Hollywood when I was working there. One of their daughters and one of my twins were roommates at the Chadwick School in Palos Verdes. Sam was the head of one of the biggest agencies there. Mildred was a very active promoter of the art museum. They both loved and collected pictures. When I stayed with them on return trips to Hollywood I discovered Sam every morning set his breakfast tray in front of one of his pictures in order to enjoy and study it. That's the kind of collectors they are. In those days Sam as an agent was a creative one. When he had an idea for a picture or someone brought him one, he would from among his clients interest a writer, a director, a star, and gathering it all together sell it as a whole to a studio. Then the whole pattern changed. A star gathered people around him to make a 'package,' raise the money and produce it independently; the agent was no longer a creator so Sam sold his agency. He and Mildred moved to London. Now he does a picture on his own when and only if an idea appeals to him. He did *Born Free*, that beautiful story of Elsa, the lion, and the picture was his, every aspect of it. As to their own pictures, almost the whole of their magnificent collection was stolen a few years ago in London. There was a lot of publicity about it. They got back the pictures but they never wanted to have them on the walls again. They felt a sense of violation, of despoilage. So some of them are stored and others are being and have been given to museums. Mildred is the polestar for all of this, and Sam knows it. She is warm and wise and humorous and unassertive, but oh my, is she steadfast in her values and in her relationships. Now, have I oversold them?"

Harvey shook his head. "I want to meet them," he said.

"I'll tell you one more thing. Sam's parents were simple Russian immigrants. He neither suppresses nor exploits that background. How's that for quality?"

"I want to meet them," Biffy said. I hadn't known she had been listening.

The rain came on full strength before we reached Athlone. In spite of that, Biffy, Lloyd and Sophy, when we had docked, went for a walk. Sophy was in a costume she had not before revealed to us and some of us felt would have been more happily left at the bottom of her bag. Others maintained its appearance was a highlight of the trip. Lloyd, asked to agree with this opinion, answered judicially—that is, cautiously.

"Well, it *is* a very baby blue," and after a pause, "I'll enjoy walking with you."

It was indeed a very baby blue and from a hood tied under her chin by a drawstring, a bulky zippered jacket also tied round the bottom with a drawstring, and voluminous trousers tied around each ankle with a drawstring, it covered her. I cannot give dimensions to prove her suede fleece-lined boots were unnaturally large; they seemed to be.

There was no reservation about Biffy's enthusiasm. "It's the prettiest outfit I've ever seen," she said. "Come on. I can't wait for other people to see it."

The General accepted with pleasure the enthusiasm and the derision.

"I like it," she said with decorous simplicity, smoothing down the front of the garment, and then we saw the costume included mittens to match. At the door she turned back to wave goodbye. The room seemed darker when she had gone.

There was a noticeable change of spirit on their return an hour or so later. They called attention to it themselves. "I am disgruntled," Sophy announced. "That's what I am. Disgruntled."

"I'm chagrined," Lloyd volunteered. "That's what I am. Chagrined."

A sudden wild recollection came to me, of my twins at the age of five in a performance of *A Midsummer Night's Dream*, reciting "I'm Peaseblossom," "I'm Mustardseed."

Biffy was saying, "I'm triumphant."

"And a little smug?" Harvey inquired, eyeing her appraisingly. What a sharp eye the man had.

Biffy admitted this with a nod. While Albert and Harvey, like pages attending a knight, were ridding Sophy of her costume, she protesting, "This is even more disgruntling," and Biffy and Lloyd shedding raincoats and hats—for some time after, we had to step over puddles at that end of the room—the travelers explained, talking across one another. Sophy had seen a sweets shop that was open and wanted to make a few purchases there. Sophy made herself heard: "I wanted to slip in by myself, without anyone noticing me," and had the grace to look embarrassed at the response from her audience.

"We had scattered as usual," Biffy had now taken over,

"looking into various shopwindows at different ends of the street, but wherever Sophy was she was not unnoticed. I followed because I wanted to see what was open, and Lloyd came in a minute or two later. There were several people in the shop and Sophy was in the middle of them. The other customers and the saleslady were giving advice and asking to help. Sophy was red in the face. She had got her mittens off. I saw them on the counter beside a number of packages of candies I supposed she had bought. When I joined them, she was saying,

" 'I'm frightfully sorry. I'm afraid I can't take those things after all.' Then she said like an explosion, 'I can't get my wallet out. It's in my pants pocket under my jacket. I can feel it but the drawstring's so tight I can't get up under it. I'm terribly sorry.'

"It looked to me as if she were not going to be able to get her hand out either from under the jacket.

"Then Lloyd was joining the group and he was saying, 'Just a minute, just a minute, please. Of course, I'm going to pay for the lady's sweets. I wouldn't have let her buy them anyway.'

"Then Sophy was protesting and the other customers were making noises of approval of the 'foine' gentleman and Lloyd was at the counter unbuttoning his raincoat and reaching into his pocket. Everybody watched while he reached into all his pockets, one at a time. I waited until he had turned the last one of them inside out and then I paid for the sweets."

"Oh, Lloyd," Ellen said from the couch, "you really shouldn't go out without money. Suppose you got run over, or had to take a taxi."

That night the Hacketts and I, at his request, initiated Harvey into the game of Scrabble. Harvey is a cultivated man of many parts, widely read, a distinguished architect, a beautiful watercolorist. He is not a Scrabble player. His

142

single contribution to that game is his enthusiasm. Now a player knows the letters and the words they form must interlock. Harvey's is not that method. He likes to make a word in an upper corner away from the clutter of the others. He enjoys making words, likes the look and sound of them. If he can bring them together by an attractive design of smaller words, connectives, he will pursue that plan but he is not unwilling to leave his creations in splendid isolation. This made an interesting but tiring evening.

The Hacketts' acceptance of my suggestion that we go to bed was so eager, Frances was worried. She came into my cabin when we had left the others still reading upstairs. Did I think she and Albert had let Harvey think it was because of his playing that we had stopped the game? "He's such a dear man and such a beautiful artist, I couldn't bear to have his spirit crushed." She was convinced, I think, by my assurances.

"You wait and see," I told her as she was leaving, "he'll ask to play again." He did, the following night.

Frances and Albert went shopping next morning immediately after breakfast. They had from me the location of the shop where I had bought a Waterford bowl on our first stop there. "The left side of the street," I said, "as you go into the town, this side of the Prince of Wales Hotel. You can't mistake the shop because all around the Waterford glass you'll find fishing tackle and cameras, God knows what else."

They had had no difficulty finding it, they told me on their return, and had bought a dozen Waterford liqueur glasses.

"They're for Lillian Hellman," Frances explained, "because she loaned me her fur-lined coat for this trip. I wanted something appropriate."

Everyone but Harvey had gone shopping in the town again and come back panting and laden. Sophy had bought some

144

heavenly, she said, lightweight throws in delicious colors but she had had those sent direct. The others had made smaller purchases that they carried but were panting because Maeve had said we were to make an early start. She had been on her way at half past ten to recall Anthony from his morning jar.

"It's not the jar that occupies him," she had explained. "It's the talk. He never goes into a pub no matter where it is that he doesn't run into old pals, so of course they have to have words together. He's been on this river all his life, you know."

We left Athlone at noon; the General as usual established the departure time. All morning the rain had been like a shy child at a party; you knew it was there but wouldn't come into the living room. While we were at lunch, with a rush

145

the rain joined the party and stayed. We had hoped and planned to stop again at Clonmacnoise. This had been the reason for an urgency about our so-called early departure, but we sent word by Maeve to Anthony we would not stop even for the added treat of seeing Sophy in her costume again. There was such a rightness about the change of plans, it might have been directed by the hand of God. There is a lovely Irish blessing that includes "May the rains fall soft upon your fields." The rain falling soft wrapped Clonmacnoise in a cloak. A few minutes beyond, the rain stopped and the mist lifted. We were still on deck. During the time we were passing Clonmacnoise I think no one had spoken. I think each of us felt a voice would pierce and shatter that floating image. Now it was Clonmacnoise again, a group of strong and enduring shafts well planted in the ground and sharply defined in the air. We took off our rain gear—Sophy was wearing a conventional raincoat and hat —we spread it to dry over railings and chair backs and came inside. The chairs and deck were too wet for sitting. Everyone was restless—no, not everyone. Harvey was at his table capturing in watercolors the magic islands that Clonmacnoise had made in the mist. He was preoccupied totally, I could see as I passed him—I realized I was passing other people too. No one had settled down to a book—or postcards; usually, I remembered, indoors, we were a settled lot. My own impatience was for the Jaffes' arrival and a certain anxiety about their finding us. No matter how much I derided it, I could not shake off a sense of personal responsibility for things going smoothly. Evidently this was not the reason for the aimless activity of the others. When Biffy said:

"Isn't this ridiculous, that I feel like a child coming back for the summer to a place he has spent the summer before?" There was general rueful agreement. She amplified, "I think it's partly because when we got to Banagher we had settled in. The first night on the cruise I think we were finding our way."

Frances added, "And one another, don't you think?"

Biffy nodded. "But at Banagher we'd stopped being over-considerate and felt free to step out on our own. I want to see again the place where Harvey and I danced."

Harvey, brush in hand, looked across at her from his studio. "So do I," he said. "That was a highlight."

"Until two o'clock in the morning," was Sophy's comment.

Ignoring this, Biffy was talking to Harvey. "Of course, the caravan will have gone ["Please God," was my interjection] and the lights and the tent. But we can see where it was."

Maeve ran through the room, high heels tapping on the floor.

"We're coming into Banagher," she called back. As Biffy had said, like children we hurried after her, calling out to one another as remembered things came into view.

"Here's the bridge. We'll go under it."

"There's the place we bought the sweaters."

"Our dance hall's just up the road."

Even though I knew that voice I had to verify it, because it was hard to believe anything could have coaxed Harvey from his base. He was standing behind me, indicating with a paintbrush the little dirt road that led up the hill to the highway. By the time we had tied up, Harvey had cleaned his brushes, emptied his glasses of water, closed his studio for the night. Like Jack and Jill, Harvey and Biffy went up the hill hand in hand, promising to return soon so as to be on deck for the Jaffes' arrival. I took as a personal favor from the Deity the beneficence that the rain had stopped, the air was soft, and I thanked Him for it.

Only the General would have noted the time at the moment of the Jaffes' arrival. We were, as my father used to say, "full strength of the company," and one of that number called, "Look."

We saw a shining black limousine come slowly down the hill on the dirt road. We watched it stop alongside the strip of meadow that separated us from the road, a trimly uniformed chauffeur leave the car, remove and place together handsome pieces of luggage, extend a hand to a couple in chic traveling clothes descending from the car, and we might have been playing the children's game of Still Pond, no more moving. We were a little daft, I think, and I think it was because for a week we had seen donkey carts, horse-drawn wagons, a few passenger cars, these small and shabby, and people wearing like us whatever the weather required. We were expecting the Jaffes. We had been waiting for them, and yet when this vehicle and its occupants came toward us, it was from another world and at the moment a strange one. We were suddenly shy. Not the General. In that moment of suspended animation and silence she called,

"Hello, darlings. It's exactly half past four."

That brought us out of our catatonic seizure. Everyone moved, Sophy and I in the lead. Maeve was ahead of us by way of the outside passage. Mr. Kearsley rose up from the meadow or somewhere. They took from the chauffeur bags and wraps. While we were exchanging incoherently a happy greeting, he backed and turned with considerable difficulty and, disappearing over the top of the hill, took away with him that other world.

Almost from the moment he stepped from the tiny gangplank to the deck, Sam was like a child turned loose in F. A. O. Schwarz's toy shop. Taking off his coat, recognizing on the instant the bench on which to toss it, he was asking questions and answering them, at the same time acknowledging introduction to the Stevensons and joyously embracing the Hacketts and the Garrisons.

148

"Is this where you sit and read or talk in the evenings or when you come indoors? Do you call it the lounge? Look, Mildred, this is where we can sit indoors. It's called a lounge. Are those tables desks where you can write letters or whatever? Mildred, aren't those desks convenient? Is that where you work, Mr. Stevenson? They told me you were a painter. Mildred, that's where Mr. Stevenson works. He's doing watercolors. I want to look at them as soon as you'll show them to me. Is this end the dining room? You sit at these tables. I never imagined there would be so much space. It's so big. Mildred, you never imagined this would be so roomy. Is the kitchen beyond? What is it they call it on boats? The galley. Maybe I'll get to be a seafaring man and call it the galley. Mildred, look at this compact kitchen. You call it a galley when you're on a boat. Is that a serving pantry? No, it's a bar. It's well stocked too." He was taking a quick look around the shelves. "Room for a bartender on one side. If my guess is right, that will be Sophy—and everybody else on the other."

"Sam," Mildred was calling from the head of the stairs, "come down and see where we sleep. We've got separate cabins, you and I." She had not been within hearing of Sam's self-guided tour. Following Maeve, who was carrying some of the bags, she had gone immediately to see their sleeping accommodations and was gratifyingly pleased with them. From habit of personal responsibility I allowed myself a deep sigh of relief and again thanked the Deity. Following Sam, we crowded down the stairs and into the narrow corridor below.

Mildred is what I have heard called in the theater "a quick study." She had already learned from Maeve the arrangement and occupants of every cabin and pointed these out to Sam. When I reached her she drew me by my hand, squeezing it, into her own cabin.

149

"I haven't seen Sam like this for years." And her eyes were shining. "I'd almost forgotten how he used to be. I thought we were just getting old and serious but look at him, listen to him. I'll never be able to thank you enough."

"Darling," I protested, "we haven't even started."

"It's the beginning that counts," was her answer. She nodded with put-on solemnity. "You'll see."

When I came from Mildred's room into the corridor, the group had scattered but at the doorway to one of the two johns Lloyd and Albert were standing on either side of Sam. They were giving him instructions and Albert was saying, "Now, Sam, to flush it, you have to pump that handle you see over there and pump it hard. When you hear it saying to you, 'Brooklyn, Brooklyn, Brooklyn,' you know it's going great and you stop."

"Now that's a funny thing," Lloyd answered. Head on one side, he was nodding contemplatively. "To me, it says, 'New York Times, New York Times.'" As I went upstairs they were debating which phrase would come more clearly to Sam and he was assuring them he would try both. Summoned to tea and fresh hot teacakes, he was almost reduced to a silence of bliss and contentment. After expressing this he only sighed from time to time. Mildred had a chance to speak and took it.

"I might as well tell you," she confided, "I've had a few misgivings but I began to lose them when I stepped on board, and when I got downstairs and saw everybody had a cabin and one left over to store your bags, I could have purred."

"There are flaws, Mildred," Albert told her anxiously.

"Name one," was Mildred's challenge and Albert took it up without hesitation.

"Towels," he said. "This is the summer of the cold, damp towel and not just Irish towels. We had a house on the Vineyard for two months this summer, and I never once put my face into a really dry towel."

150

Sam entered or reentered the conversation. "Mildred," he said, "I've been thinking and I've got a great idea."

"Oh, God," Mildred told him, "I knew this was going to happen but not so soon."

"Wouldn't it be great to have a boat just like this and bring the kids and the grandchildren? We'd just mosey along, stop now and then, do some fishing."

"I have never fished in my life and neither have you," Mildred reminded him.

Sam brushed this aside. "The kids might like it or maybe friends. We've probably got a hundred friends who would give anything in the world to go on a boat like this and have some fishing."

"A little crowded," Mildred suggested, "and not an extra cabin for the bags."

"And we'd go up to the village to market every day and come home with a big basket of fresh vegetables and fruit like the people we saw in the village as we came through."

"I wish you'd brought some with you," Harvey said wistfully. "We haven't had any."

"And fresh fish right out of the river." Sam did not even hear the interruptions. "Oh I tell you it will be a wonderful life. You're going to love it, Mildred."

"Oh but Sam, dear." Ellen's voice trembled a little. "I really don't think Mildred would be happy with a hundred people all fishing and carrying market baskets and washing so many dishes. Of course, Lloyd is wonderful about washing dishes in the country and we do put beautiful music on our record player while we're in the kitchen but this is a very small kitchen and it can be very boring if you don't like music."

Mildred leaned across the table to pat Ellen's arm. "Not to worry," she said.

# 12

Next morning we were not up with the lark. The evening had been late and gala. At a moment when no one was looking, and this would have been hard to find, Sam had slipped to Maeve two bottles of champagne. As soon as the first was brought in and the cries of astonishment had subsided, Sam had risen to his feet, saying these were the people with whom he and Mildred wanted most to be on this day, their forty-fifth wedding anniversary, and adding now that he had come aboard and seen his surroundings this was the place in which he most wanted to be.

Mildred inserted audibly, "No, Sam, it's never the place that matters. It's always the people."

This reduced us all to a moist sentimentality, Harvey accepts with charming grace chaffing from his friends about his emotional susceptibility. He and Biffy had met the Jaffes only two hours earlier, but at the conclusion of Sam's little speech and Mildred's postscript, Harvey's eyes were not the only eyes brimming; he was not chaffed.

The General is one of a family of speechmakers. It is said

with some exaggeration that when even two of its members dine together each makes a speech to the other. I had known without looking, Sam and Mildred had provided an opening into which Sophy would dive. I had not been mistaken. That was how the evening had begun and it had continued like the champagne, live and sparkling. We had pressed the Jaffes to tell us about their Russian trip since under the auspices of the Tate Gallery in London it had provided admission to art treasures not on public view. We had asked Sam to talk about the filming of his beautiful picture *Born Free* and the new one he was working on. It had been an evening to remember, we had agreed, and it had been a late one.

At breakfast I explained to the newcomers the way we had learned to order and what they might expect because they would not be given a choice. The only decision put to them would be whether or not they wanted fruit juice. If they declined, Maeve would answer, "Ah, then you just want breakfast."

The breakfast would be eggs and a rasher of bacon they would call it, but actually it would be much more like our slice of ham, and I warned them:

"For heaven's sakes, look out for the dark places on the rasher. Those will be solid bone and tooth-crackers."

With eggs on another day there would be sausages that would look like miniature hot dogs, a delicacy I happened to dislike with venom. I would have pushed these aside but my childhood training has never died. In the tradition of "Eat everything on your plate or no dessert" and "You will at least taste it no matter if it's different and you don't like its looks," I did taste the sausages, and asked for more.

So I told Sam if it should happen to be sausage that morning not to be put off by its looks. It would be delicious. Instead of eggs there might be broiled tomatoes and there would always be the Irish toast that had become a total diet breakdown, a foundering for all of us. As I was concluding these introductions, Maeve came from the kitchen followed by an attractive young dark-eyed girl.

"This is Anita," Maeve told us. "She'll be with us now till the end of the cruise to help me."

Mr. Kearsley was close on her heels. I had to believe, for the sake of sanity, there must be a door from the galley to the outer corridor. Three people could not possibly have been hidden in that small room. I would have liked to ask when and how Mr. Kearsley had signed on Anita and brought her aboard without our knowing, but I decided at the same moment I would rather not know. If Mr. Kearsley's appearances were always without any indication of his approaching, why not Anita's?

Mr. Kearsley had come to tell us a bus had been ordered to drive us to Clonfert. Ellen had diffidently suggested the excursion, and been taken aback by our eager acceptance. "Because you were so right about Birr," Sophie explained. Sam asked what time we should be ready and I shook my head at him. There were still things he needed to learn.

St. Brendan's Cathedral is at Clonfert and had it taken us five times longer than the hour in the bus I would have counted the trip well worth making, and not one of our group would have challenged me. St. Brendan, according to the things written about him, was a roving fellow and an adventurer. One of the first chronicles of his life, called *Navigatio Rendani,* was written in Latin in the ninth century. According to this chronicle the bold Abbot with a party of monks left the coast of Kerry on a journey called "Peregrinatio," which means a voluntary exile that was one of the "ascetical practices" of the age of saints. On this voyage he and his companions had encountered a whale (landing on it, having mistaken it for an island), an iceberg, a volcano

154

in eruption, and eventually reached the promised land of saints. It was later identified as America (never say to an Irishman that America was discovered by another than St. Brendan). Returning from this penitential excursion, and there is no evidence that he was in any way diminished by it, he founded a monastery at Clonfert in 558 A.D. I quote from the pamphlet on Clonfert: "The Rule dictated to him, it is said, by an angel was so highly esteemed that it continued to be observed for centuries after his death. He died

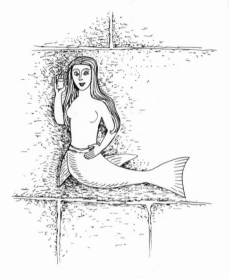

in 578. He was absent from the monastery at the time but a belief continues that his body was brought back to Clonfert and put in a grave never identified. The Monastery of Clonfert expanded to become the great College of St. Brendan, housing some 3,000 students. In the reign of Queen Elizabeth it was a rival of Trinity College, Dublin, for the royal seal and designation of 'The University' but Dublin won over Clonfert."

For those of us who are not scholars of history, architecture and archeology, but who come to enjoy and remember, the rewards here are in the magnificent west doorway, the exquisite east window and the enchanting Mermaid. The Mermaid is a small carved figure "in the south side of the chancel arch." She dates from the fifteenth century and is a symbol of the story that St. Brendan on his great voyage preached to the creatures of the sea. Since I am not a scholar and therefore not under the restraint of considered judgment or phraseology, I can and do say the Mermaid is a creature of utter enchantment arousing in that holy place shameful covetousness.

Finally and not in order of importance on the list of things to see and remember at Clonfert is the Yew Walk and I defy anyone to stand at its entrance, walk its length and, returning home, have to be reminded of the way it looks. The trees themselves are said to be over a thousand years old. They meet overhead in a high Gothic arch and beneath it twenty people could walk abreast. It might be the center aisle of a great cathedral. Things that I shall remember about it are sunlight through the leaves making a mosaic on the ground, and that, walking its length and back, we were the only ones there. Lloyd said:

"This is a holy place."

The bus driver had joined us on our tour of Clonfert, admitting he had never been there before though he lived less than twenty miles distant. He was young, eager, enthusiastic and intuitively perceptive of our interests.

As we were leaving Clonfert, this young man said he wanted to ask something. He began again to speak, stammered, stopped, hesitated. We could see the back of his neck turning deep red. We encouraged him to tell us what it was and he was finally able to be articulate, although in the telling of it by jerks and pauses his embarrassment was so great, his driving coinciding with his speech was convulsively in jerks and stops.

156

Finally I, always craven in a car, urged him to stop until he had told us what he wanted. He agreed because, he said, we were there anyway. We might like to pause here, he said, since it would not be out of our way more than a little, to see Our Lady of Clonfert. My heart sank because he was pointing to a small modern and bleak little church, its exterior covered in a plaster of muddy yellow. I thought we must go inside but what could we possibly say to him that

would not hurt his feelings, because he had shown himself at Clonfert so intuitive, he would sense our distaste. I felt quite sick as I got out of the car; talking later with one another about this miracle of the day, we admitted each one of us had had precisely those feelings.

We followed him up a gravel path trying to find something to admire. He was not listening to us. He pushed up ahead, opened the inner door and then stood back to give us a clear view of the center aisle. There at its end was one of the most beautiful figures of a madonna I have ever seen. She is a painted wooden figure of the fourteenth century done by local craftsmen. What we knew then was that she was warm and gentle, that in the painted face were tenderness and understanding, and that her robe of heavenly blue was so beautifully draped, its folds might have been done in satin or velvet. The bodice beneath the robe was in a delicate soft rose, and the curious headdress with a veil that reached almost to her waist was as soft in texture as the garments. The infant Jesus seated on her curved right arm was stiff, unnatural, a little grotesque, consistent with the period.

When, leaving, we thanked our driver; I hope he was not suspicious of our over-eager acceptance of his suggestion we go from there to Cloghan. It was a castle, he told us, and he'd learned the day before it would be open because the contents were about to be auctioned, the property that had been in one family for many generations had gone out of the family and was now being sold. What the smell of smoke is to an old firehorse, the words "auction" and "furniture" are to Ellen and me. They would have lured us to a detour however wide. Also, after being led to Our Lady of Clonfert, we might be shown the Holy Grail. We would follow our driver anywhere.

The end of this excursion was not the Holy Grail but it was quite an experience. We drove into a wide courtyard bricked-faced and, beyond, a grim, sizable but not castle-size house of gray stones. As we got out of the car the front door opened and a man wearing a tweed jacket and corduroy trousers came out. He carried a rifle and was followed by two dogs that at sight of us crouched and growled. We backed away a little but I, prompted by a sense of personal responsibility I cannot shake off, became the spokesman.

"We have been told," I said, with false assurance, "there is to be an auction of furnishings tomorrow and we would be enormously interested in seeing them if you would permit it."

He bared his teeth like one of the dogs and said, grinding his molars between words:

"The viewing will be tomorrow, the auction on the following day; you might have taken notice of this since it has been in every paper all over the countryside. It was arranged by the auctioneers who have swarmed over my house for two weeks like a band of Palestinian guerrillas."

Responsible or not, I was more than ready to call it a day and leave with a prayer the dogs or the man would not attack us before we could get back into the car. Ellen, who has a determination many gentle people, I have discovered, possess, rallied. With, to me, endearing persuasive charm she told him that we could not possibly be there on the following day because we were cruising on a boat and must leave that afternoon.

The owner said, "I couldn't possibly care less. Goodbye."

The only part of the episode for which I was profoundly thankful was that, returning to the house, he took the dogs with him. Driving away, we interrupted our driver's almost tearful apologies. Now that we were safely back in the car we assured him we'd rather enjoyed the incident. Only Ellen, murmuring wistfully, had wanted to see the interior and the furniture and perhaps if she had tried once more she might have persuaded him. A chorus of gratitude to Ellen for not trying again silenced her.

Because, I suppose, of my "satiable curtiosity" I asked the driver to tell us the story of the irascible gentleman whose castle we had invaded. Our young man, with obvious and commendable restraint—and good manners—said the gentleman was not a popular figure in the countryside; after a pause elaborating. If he caught anyone just walking on any part of his 150 acres of property he immediately went out with his dogs and the gun and shot over the head of the

159

trespasser. It was understood he was going back to England. "Likely he'll be better understood there."

I wondered aloud what his lady was like.

The nice young man, looking straight ahead, answered, "She's just like him."

The General said hesitantly she would like to make a suggestion. Since it is so unlike the General to be hesitant, we gave her astonished, concentrated attention. Because we had spent less time at Cloghan than we had anticipated—a triumph of understatement if ever I heard one—could we go instead to Shannon Harbour? I was the only one who laughed and I explained immediately why and that it was affectionate laughter.

From the moment of planning, of thinking about the trip, Sophy, I told them, had yearned to go to Shannon Harbour. That would be as close as we could come to traveling on the Grand Canal. She had shown it to me on the map, drawing a pencil along its length, a necessary amplification because I am incapable of reading or understanding maps. I regret this limitation and am a little ashamed of it but now I accept it. I have been with her on canals in England and in France and I share her love of them but my disappointment had not been so acute when we learned the Grand Canal was no longer navigable. She had wanted to follow at least part of the course of that great wave of emigration to America. Thwarted in this, she had said she would be partly reconciled if she could see Shannon Harbour. Sophy is a skilled maneuverer. This is one of the essential attributes of a general and this one was one of her best. I read later there was nothing of interest to see, only old warehouses, a dismantled hotel and the canal fallen into disuse. We found this not at all true. The old warehouses were quite beautiful and there were dwellings alongside we found charming. The frame of the big hotel is there, a beautiful Georgian building, and the overall air of sadness is in keeping with its story. Emigrants to America had come there by horse-drawn canal-boats from Dublin. They stayed overnight, sometimes longer, for a connection with the next lap of the long journey into exile. There were banquets and dances and festivities in the hotel to ease the anguish of the separation, in most cases for a lifetime. From Shannon Harbour the passengers went by coach, mostly to Limerick, from there they took ship to New York or Philadelphia, or Boston. Some time later when that tidal wave of emigration had receded, the Grand Hotel had so few guests it was partially dismantled to avoid the payment of taxes. The inside was gutted and the roof taken off but the beautiful outer form is there.

We were back in Banagher in time to allow Sam and Mildred, guided by Ellen and Lloyd, to visit the local craft shop across the road where the men had bought sweaters and accessories. Mildred wanted very much to buy an Irish sweater. When they returned Lloyd was wearing a new sweater and Sam immediately put on his new one. Neither Ellen nor Mildred had made a purchase. The purpose of an Irish sweater is to keep its wearer comfortable in the roughest weather. Sam was so pleased with his purchase he did not accept the suggestion that he take it off inside. Later he admitted, "It does get the steam up and every now and then I have to go on deck to ventilate."

Harvey naturally was the first to see the double rainbow. Though we were having lunch, the fact that we were in motion made it necessary for him to divide his attention between the food and the passing scene. When we traveled and ate simultaneously as we did only occasionally, he sat by a window that looked forward. A provocative sight ahead would take him at a rush to his paints. At our delightful rate of speed it was easily possible for him to catch the scene on paper by the time we had caught up with and passed it.

161

When he saw the rainbows and cried out his discovery it had not been raining. The air was misty but clear and there they were on the horizon, two perfect arches, shimmering in the mist, now bright in color, then fading. It was a long time before they faded out. We called it a good omen and it was, for weather and sights ahead.

During lunch we had been talking about the feeling we had shared at Shannon Harbour, that we had walked into the past, that perhaps ghosts of emigrants came home to dance in the hotel at night, and strange things might happen to an intruder. Lloyd was reminded of and told a story he had read a night or two before in a book about Yeats. Yeats himself had told the story of a man and his servant girl and Yeats had known the man to whom this had happened. The servant girl had come to the master as he was dressing to go on a journey and at sight of him had cried out:

"You musn't put that shirt on. It's got blood on it."

She took it off and brought him another that he put on. He went on his trip and was shot. When the servant went to get the original shirt he had not worn, in order to wash it, she could not find a trace of blood on it and, Lloyd added, Yeats maintained this was a true story. In the silence that followed, Ellen spoke.

"But Lloyd dear," she said, "why was the man shot?"

Sam was the one who announced our arrival at Portumna. There was still an hour or two to go before he and Mildred would have been on the boat twenty-four hours, but he had become vocally very nautical, if inaccurate. He had designated Albert as the mate, and so, the recipient of his requests and demands, and Albert had signed on willingly. Since the Garrisons, the Stevensons and Sophy were actual and competent sailors, Sam was aware of this instinctively. They were not included in the nautical exchange, but we all heard Sam call to Albert:

162

"Port the helm, mate, we're coming about, latitude by starboard."

I hoped Anthony had not heard him.

We were about three quarters of a mile from the town, Maeve told us as she was tying up, and why Sam was not caught in a noose I cannot explain, because he was directly in the way of the rope, watching with delight every move she made, and calling to Mildred to come and see her dexterity.

Some of our company, Sam included, went off at once to explore. Sophy said it was exactly ten minutes to four and they would be back for tea. Mildred and I stayed on the boat for a catching up. We would visit the town in the morning.

That evening and night are marked in my memory by the introduction of the others to a game Sophy and I knew, and by a disturbance in the night; the game came first. I suggested it immediately after dinner. I think in the back of my mind was the possibility that Harvey might want to play scrabble.

Our game may have another name. I know it as the Telephone Game, I told them, when they had all acquiesced eagerly to my suggestion, and this in itself was unusual because in my experience in a group there are almost bound to be one or two members at least who loathe any game.

As I explained, Sophy and I were distributing paper and pencils. Down the margin of the page I told them to write the letters of the alphabet, one underneath the other, allowing space in between for as many names as would come to mind.

"Then one of us will give a letter and in the next ten minutes you must write, like a listing in the telephone book, the last name and the first name—and there's the rub—of a famous person, at least one who should be known to all of us. For instance, suppose the letter B is given. I think of Beethoven, but it's not enough for me to write down Beethoven. I must give his first name, Ludwig Beethoven, and I put it under the letter L, not B, because the whole page with that alphabet is going to be taken up by this single letter, whichever one is given, so I would put Charlotte Brontë under C and, hopefully, other C.B.'s like Charles Beard, Constance Bennett, and so on. At the end of ten minutes when time is called, the person who gave the letter reads off the names he has put down. If no one else has that name and if it is accepted, he marks himself ten for that. If someone else has thought of the same one, he gives himself five and the other one takes five. If more than two have the same name, each one gets three and obviously the one with the highest score wins."

There were a few questions of details and then we began. It was a longer and more animated single round of that game than I have ever experienced, not so much in the game itself, though the time limit was greeted with cries of anguish and entreaties to extend it, but in the scoring. For every person of the theater on his list Albert, leaping to his feet, gave an animated characterization, of such distinction we begged for an encore and he obliged. I had expected challenges. This always occurs in that game but I had not reckoned on Sam's fervor. We had met and dealt with Harvey's defense of architects, Lloyd's of ballplayers and distinguished Harvard athletes, conceding some, flouting others, but we were unanimous in a denial of one of Sam's candidates, Marvin Josephson.

"Never heard of him," we said.

Sam was aghast, his voice, rising to an unnatural height, trembled. "Never heard of him!" he repeated. "He's the president of C.M.A."

Only the Hacketts had heard of that and apologized to Sam for our ignorance.

"You must remember, Sam dear, we're the only theater people in this group. They really wouldn't know Creative Managers Association."

Sam was mollified. "If I tell you he has just bought for three million dollars the exclusive television rights to the Olympics, will you say you don't know who he is?"

We conceded to Sam he was probably a very famous person and not to know about him was revealing our own ignorance, nevertheless we stood firm.

Sam delivered his final thrust:

"If you don't accept him, Marvin Josephson is going to be very offended."

# 13

When the call from Sam rang through the downstairs corridor the next morning at about eight o'clock some of us were at breakfast, others were still in their cabins.

"Ahoy! Avast! Would Claudette Colbert count double for two C's?"

"No," we chorused and resumed our occupations.

"I went to sleep thinking names," Sam told us at the breakfast table. "I'm in great shape for the game tonight. Where do we go today?"

Sophy, diverted from her breakfast, looked up at him ironically.

"And where were you," she wanted to know, "last night during the shooting? Playing the Telephone Game to yourself?"

The full strength of the company was by this time assembled and set up an incoherent clamor of "What shooting? When? Where was it?"

Sophy and I made an antiphonal chorus of explanation and chiding. Each of us had been wakened at around two o'clock by shouts and then shots, finally a tremendous splash. It had been terrifying. As far as we knew somebody had been murdered and thrown into the river. Meeting in the corridor we realized we were the only ones who had heard it, since no one else was stirring. We had stayed downstairs, each of us pretty shaky, we admitted, unwilling to investigate above and perhaps be a target.

Our recital brought forth protests of dismay, some dis-belief, reproaches that we had not summoned help, and finally the realization that, other than the Hacketts, ours were the only sleeping accommodations on that side of the boat. The others were all on the opposite side and the Hacketts self-admittedly were somewhat deaf. We had finally gone back to our respective beds and eventually to sleep.

We were still discussing possible explanations and refuting indignantly some implied and expressed skepticism, when Harvey, looking out the window as usual, told us a man was coming across the meadow from another estuary on its op-posite side and seemed to be heading for our boat. Some of us went out on deck at the moment he reached it, surprising him as he was calling, "Hallo, hallo." He was obviously startled at our sudden appearance simultaneously with his call, and embarrassed. It was obvious too that he was German and spoke very little English. He had come, he made us understand, to apologize and explain about a happening of the night before. He and a party of friends had chartered a boat for duck shooting. Last night they had gone to a pub and got very drunk. Coming home from the village, they had fired a few shots in the air. "Not people, joost air—in the fun." In the fun, one of them, over-exuberant, had fallen off the bridge. That was the reason for the splashing and the shouting.

Ellen interrupted him.

"I hope he's not still in the water," she suggested with anxiety. It was now half past eight.

167

*"Nein,"* was the ambiguous answer, given with a deep bow. "I am so sorry. He is in boat now. I am sorry. Goodbye."

At the sound of a new and foreign voice, the rest of our company had left the breakfast table to join us, and by the end of the recital we were full strength, including Maeve and Anita. Sophy and I led the return to breakfast, accepting graciously and modestly, I thought, apologies for previous doubts, and praise for our fortitude.

Immediately after breakfast we had an executive session with Sophy. She is the Banker as well as the General—and the Bartender. As the Banker she had learned we would find a bank here in Portumna where we could cash travelers' checks. In the role of General she told us she thought we must make our final payment to Mr. Kearsley, reminding us that since our initial advance we' had made no further payment. I interrupted her.

"I've spoken to him about this more than once. He's not easy to catch and you can guess what he has said each time. 'Time enough.' " There was smiling agreement around the circle.

"Just the same," Sophy continued, "we've really got to pin him down and persuade him to accept payment." Then, as the Banker, "I've got it all written down, what everybody owes, including the liquor, and it's understood we divide that equally." Nods of agreement again. On every trip it has been a by-now established custom—and there has never been an objection voiced—to pay for extras from a general purse. This eliminates the trying pettiness of "You had Scotch and I only had vermouth," or in restaurants, "Now how many desserts were there and how many coffees?" Instead each member puts in the pot the same amount as his neighbor. The Banker takes charge and gives word when the pot is running low and needs replenishment. The Banker for this special overall payment, had prepared—and there should be stars in her crown for this—a separate list for each of us, tabulating what was still due on the chartering of the boat from single members, and couples.

Pocketing our expense shares, we left the boat as usual singly or in clumps. I overheard Ellen cautioning Lloyd, "I know we'll get separated because you will wander and I think that's a lovely way to see things but here is our account and you *will* go to the bank, won't you?" Lloyd assured her he had no intention of wandering that day for birds or any other purpose and would certainly go to the bank and would probably be with her all the time anyway.

Nevertheless when I reached the cattle market, Lloyd was there and Albert, but no sign of Ellen. My route had been anything but direct. I had been to the bank, seen several of my friends there, done my business and gone my own way, meandering with deep pleasure along rows of little houses each with a tiny garden in front ablaze with autumn bloom and nearly every one displaying plants in its front windows. Later I read in Leonard Wibberley's *The Shannon Sailors*— and I hope everyone who may see this will rush out to share my enjoyment of that delightful and delicious book—"Portumna is the prettiest little town you are likely to find in a day's travel. It has, to be sure, the gray cast of all Irish towns from the use of limestone for building material. But there are dabs of flowers here and there in tubs and windowboxes, and clean streets and painted windows and doors, bright and cheerful." That is exactly the way I found it.

When Lloyd and Albert joined me, though I had not known of its existence, I had found the cattle market. It was a surprise to them, too. I was talking to a gentleman who may have held an official position there because certainly he had wide knowledge that he gave generously. In spite of my burning curiosity about people, I am usually shy in my approach. I had lost my shyness in Ireland because universally I had

169

found such friendly outgoing interest. The gentleman was telling me, as Lloyd and Albert reached us, that cattle is in his opinion the number-one industry in Ireland, that its principal outlet "on the hoof" was England and that dressed beef went to America. After a pause for introductions, he continued. The expectation among cattle breeders was that the industry was going to soar because, by the rules of the Common Market, seventeen percent of the import tax to Germany would be removed. Their rival in importance had been tourism but that was in a bad slump now because the English would not come to Ireland. The party for the United Republic was so strong it would not allow publicity or propaganda suggesting that one might come happily and easily to Southern Ireland, enjoying all its special facilities—because that would suggest division in the country.

My new acquaintance asked if we would like to go inside to the auction and led the way, pausing at cattle pens outside. He called our attention to a white identifying label on each animal. It had been applied on the rump like a postage stamp. For a few minutes more we stayed to watch carts drive up, cattle unloaded and stamped. I paused again before we reached the auction room in order to jot down a menu for lunch, hand-printed on a sizable poster and tacked on an outside wall. It seemed a proper meal for a man who had probably been on the road since before daybreak. It read: "Oxtail Soup, Roast Beef, Cabbage, Turnip, Potatoes, Custard and Apples, Tea and Biscuits."

On two sides of the auction room tiers of seats went from floor to roof. Opposite these were the auction stand and pens. As each animal was brought in, he was weighed in front of us and his weight announced and recorded. We left after a few minutes of the auction proper. It sounded exactly like the commercial on the old Lucky Strike radio program—gibberish. I tried to find my guide again to thank him but

170

perhaps it was just as well I could not because I think he would have been astonished and disappointed that I had not enjoyed it.

Heading for home—that is, in its general direction—we meandered. There had been a good many people on the streets because this was market day, but beyond the outskirts walking along the road we met only a few; each of these spoke. Passing a little wayside country store, I suggested we stop. It had become a habit to explore any possibility for fresh fruit; I also needed Kleenex and other sundries. As we went in I said my list was consistent with the variety of merchandise we had seen in most stores. This one was no exception. The range was wide; the range of the proprietor's knowledge of arithmetic was limited. He had great difficulty adding up the total of purchases we had made, scowling and muttering as he wet his pencil for a fresh try after an erasure. At my companions' diffident offer of assistance he pushed to them eagerly the smudged, almost transparent by now, scrap of paper he'd been working on. (I had some misgivings since I happened to know that in the Hackett and Garrison families the wives do most of the adding up.) When the transaction was completed, the amount paid, proper change returned, the storekeeper was his genial self again, all anxiety erased.

"God bless," he called to us as we left the shop.

We had not shared the cattlemen's lunch. We were on the *St. Patrick* in time for our own, and it was not so different. We began with oxtail soup, went on to Irish stew (a separate dish of it done for the Hacketts and me because we are made embarrassingly ill by onions or garlic) rich with carrots and the inevitable potatoes. For dessert, there was blackberry pie. Maeve and Anita had picked the blackberries, ripe and luscious, along the road while we were in the town. We ate every bit of it plus a little Irish bread on the side. It could

171

well be that my female companions, eating this, had the same thought as I, that if we were at home we would be getting a little cheese, salad and Ry-Krisp out of the icebox, and like me, banished the thought immediately.

We were in the shameful torpor such a lunch produces when Maeve hurried through the room, her high heels like a metronome ticking her speed. Sam was on his feet at once calling out to Albert, in nautical jargon of his own invention, their help would be needed. Maeve, looking back for an instant, caught my eye and gave such a grin of enjoyment at their nonsense I laughed aloud. Mildred, looking up from her needlepoint, caught the exchange and chuckled. "Silly Sam," she said. "He knows it and he's enjoying it like a kid."

A minute or so later we heard Sam call out in a very different voice.

"Hey, what's going on here? We're sinking. Tell us *really* what to do."

Mildred was on her feet, throwing the needlepoint from her, on her way to Sam. The others, roused, were looking about in bewilderment, asking what was happening and I had difficulty making myself heard, but mine, my friends tell me, is a carrying voice.

"Hold it," I said." "We're not sinking. We're going through a lock."

Mildred sat down again and picked up her needlepoint. "Oh," she said, "not to worry."

Some of the others went out on deck with me. Sam was listening to Maeve, nodding his head as she explained what was happening. She was still talking when Sam called again.

"Mildred," he said, "come on out and watch. We're going through a lock and I want to explain to you the whole process."

She came and he explained. Maeve caught my eye again;

172

her own eyes were round with astonishment. I was close enough for her to whisper, "Will you just listen to him? He's got it perfect."

I was not surprised. "He's a good listener," I told her.

Harvey called from his studio, "What's the name of this?"

"Meelick Lock," Sam called back and Maeve shook her head.

"Now, however did he come by that?" she asked herself. "I never told him."

Our after-lunch sloth was gone. We stayed on deck, Sam still talking about the lock and the wonder of it.

"I thought the bridge that opened for us when we left Portumna was quite a sight. It's so low coming up to it you can't believe you're going to miss a crash, and then it opens at exactly the right moment. That's the kind of timing we try for in our business, isn't it, mate?"

Albert agreed.

"As a matter of fact," Sam continued ruminatively, "I don't know that I've ever gone through or under a bridge, for that matter. Over many a one in a car but I've stayed away from the water. When I was very small my mother used to take me once in a great while to Staten Island to see relatives. Before the ferry left the dock she was popping lemon drops into my mouth to keep me from being seasick—but I always was. If anyone had told me I'd be on a boat and enjoying it the way I'm enjoying this, I'd have called him a liar."

Harvey was standing in the doorway.

"I had to stop painting and look," he said. "My God, isn't it beautiful? We're out of the Shannon now, you know, into Lough Derg."

Sam looked up at him inquiringly and I hastily told him he could undoubtedly learn from Mr. Kearsley or Maeve how the Shannon became loughs and a river again but when he had found out, please not to tell me. Efforts had been made

173

and they had only increased my confusion. I begged to be allowed just to enjoy.

It was a landscape to enjoy. Mountains were rising up out of the distance on the horizon of the lough. The water between was punctuated by green islands. The afternoon was sunny and the air was soft. We tied up in the harbor of Mount Shannon along a gray stone quay and came ashore at once, scattering as usual. I think it was about four o'clock because Maeve called after us, asking if we'd be back to tea, and we told her we'd only be gone an hour or a little more.

"Time enough," she called back and waved.

The road to the village of Mount Shannon is up a hill. I was alone when I started out, but shortly after, I saw three or four of our group standing in the middle of the road looking. When I joined them I saw they had been stopped by one of the most beautiful holly trees any of us had ever seen and certainly the largest. It could have stood shoulder to shoulder with a maple. I suppose I thought of that at the time because the holly berries were scarlet and filled the tree so richly the leaves could have gone unnoticed, but not these leaves. Their green was as flaming as the red of the berries and each one of them might have been waxed and polished by someone's hand.

My first choice of all the lovely streets and roads we saw on the cruise is the main street of the village of Mount Shannon. It is broad, shaded on each side by generously proportioned trees of proud bearing. Directly across from the head of the road we had come along was a low stone house of beautiful proportions. Its façade was covered by an ivy I do not remember seeing before and cannot name. The leaves were very small and shining only a little less than those on the holly trees. The distinguishing feature of this ivy was the flatness of the vine against the house so that the whole front of the house looked like a *mille fleurs* tapestry. In its front garden a tall, large and charming topiary figure stopped us again. We kept to one side of the street and walked along it. Almost immediately we stopped at another charming house, its particular distinction a row of flower stands filled with bloom, and between every two stands, a stone urn overflowing with similar bloom. They were not part of a garden, they made a decorative and architectural frieze across the front of the house. When I crossed the street to see more closely a church on the opposite side, I realized the others had not accompanied me but I found Sophy in the adjoining cemetery. While we were looking there, we were joined by a gentleman who introduced himself as the rector and asked if we would like to see the interior of the church. He would like very much to show it to us. He did not show it to us because someone hailed from the road and he hurried off, calling back he hoped that we would wait. Innocent of what we were being spared, we did not wait for him to return.

It was a quiet little church in design and color, but the simple plaques embedded along the walls seemed, to me, banners that had been carried across the world and brought home again. I wrote down some of them. "Phillip Reade died while with his regiment at Dinapore, Bengal." On another one, "Died of wounds received in action at Battle of Arras, aged 20 years." Major Sowers died "on active service in Burma." Not far from these, a stark recital of a tragedy close to home: "In loving memory of Charles Henry Cochlan, aged 27 years, and August Irwin Cochlan, aged 25 years, the only sons of the Rev. Augustus C. L. Cochlan, rector of this parish, who were drowned in Lough Derg, on the 4th September, 1878, in consequence of their yacht Hermit having foundered in a squall. (They were medical students at Dublin University.)"

As Sophy and I came back down the hill we saw some of the others heading for the boat from the opposite direction.

175

There was nothing surprising about this because Maeve's hot teacakes were a magnet even to the bird watchers, who always went farthest afield. What was surprising was the sight of a lady waving to us from the window of a small car drawn up along the quay at the site of our boat. Mystified, we hurried to meet her. As we reached the car, its driver stepped quickly out, climbing toward us with outstretched hand. She was an elderly lady, with a spare, trim figure. Her gray hair was severely drawn to a knot at the back of her neck, but the coiffure included a winsome curl down either cheek. She introduced herself. She was Mrs. Talbot, wife of the rector of the Church of Ireland, the church we had just visited, we realized as she identified it. She wished, she said, to welcome us to Mount Shannon. She could not stay, she was on her way to a meeting in the village, but her husband, Mr. Talbot, would call on us presently. This announcement was a surprise. We had not before been called upon by the clergy, nor by anyone else for that matter. However—she was continuing—she had a few minutes and would like to take us in her car just up the hill and, she pointed, to the rectory, from which we would have the best views, she assured us, of the harbor and the countryside. Her briskness quenched our demurs and we were in her car and on our way. Looking back, I saw the later arrivals standing in a group watching us. I waved with what I hoped was a gesture saying we hoped to return soon and this was none of our doing. Later I was told my gesture conveyed absolutely nothing, only left them in a bewildered daze.

The view from Mrs. Talbot's hilltop was as splendid as she had promised and I am glad we saw it. The excursion included at her insistence a quick tour of the house, a large and quite beautiful brick residence with lovely pieces among its furnishings that we were given no time to observe in any detail, had we been inclined to linger over them, which we

176

were not. We were set down again at the boat. At the moment of unloading us she was on her way with such speed, Sophy had to run a few steps in order to shut the car door. Our friends were not particularly relieved by our return, and only moderately interested to learn where we had been and that Mr. Talbot was going to call. This lack of interest piqued me a little. I inquired sharply if it had occurred to any of them we might have been kidnaped.

"Oh no, dear," was Ellen's answer, "because, as I told the others, the driver had side curls and they were gray."

Albert was sitting by a window on the quay side. He put up a hand. "Listen," he said. "It sounds like tap dancing. What on earth?"

He stood up to get a better view and beckoned to us. There were three little people outside at the far end of the boat from us, two of them toddlers. They were sitting down playing with small pebbles. The third, the baby-sitter, a child of about seven or eight, we guessed, had evidently grown bored with her charges and their play, and was amusing herself by dancing. Albert immediately went outside and we followed. She had stopped when he reached her, but when he asked if she would repeat it, she nodded and began again. With complete self-possession and dignity she did one intricate step after another. She danced with her arms straight at her sides, the hands doubled into fists. Obviously no music was playing but her rhythm was so exact I could almost hear, even sing, the tune. Maeve came out to see what had taken us from our tea and stayed to watch with us.

"That's called step dancing," she explained to us. "She's good at it."

Sam asked if Maeve could do it.

"I can, surely," was her answer, and she went back to the kitchen. The child never spoke, only shook her head when

177

Albert in a very tactful way offered her money. She did, however, take the teacakes we offered, feeding in small pieces one to each of the babies. They were still playing when we went down later to change for dinner. While I was dressing I could hear outside my window the quick intricate taps of her dancing.

# 14

The children had gone when I came upstairs for cocktails but Frances, outside, was talking to another caller. My recognition was by stages: the clerical garb, the gentleman who had unlocked the church door—then this must be the rector and the husband of Mrs. Talbot. She had said he would call. I had no apprehension about the timing of the call. Frances knew the pattern of our day; she would not allow an intrusion into our cocktail hour, that beautiful culmination in a tradition established by Sophy on the first trip she and I, with other friends, had made.

The General's versatility in the role of bartender includes providing as well as dispensing spirits according to individual taste. When we are on a trip by land she carries the liquor in a shoebag. She knows there are bags designed for the purpose of carrying bottles but she considers these ostentatious and therefore vulgar. She substitutes a shoebag for the more stylish receptacle. Sophy is by birth a Philadelphian and occasionally this birthmark is visible. We do not like bars with their noise and elbow-rubbing proximity to neighbors; we like the privacy of a room, whichever room is the largest. This may necessitate sitting on beds, a dressing-table bench or whatever. Nevertheless we prefer it. In that sanctum Sophy, having ordered ice and whatever other incidentals are necessary, brings from the shoebag Scotch, bourbon, gin, vodka, sherry, vermouth for me, whatever the individual requirements call for. Therefore this hour is known among us as the "Shoebag Hour," and it is sacred. Some time earlier, going down to dress, Sophy had called out, "Shoebag in forty minutes?"

"Right," had come from every cabin.

At the sight of Frances and her companion, I returned quickly below to give warning.

"Frances is receiving a caller," I told them, "but bless her heart, she's keeping him outside. I'll give you the word when he's gone." I did not keep hostess and caller under actual surveillance. I went back to my cabin for a short time. Coming out again and partway up the stairs, I saw no one on the deck, heard no sound of conversation, turned back and gave the word.

"All clear."

Every door opened simultaneously. There was a rush for the stairs so that we emerged at the top almost in a body to find Frances and the clergyman sitting side by side, looking toward us expectantly.

"Ah, there you are"—an inanity so unlike her it revealed her uneasiness. "I've asked Father Talbot to come in for a glass of sherry."

The "Father" showed she was in a deplorable state of nerves. I had said "Mr. Talbot" since that was the appellation Mrs. Talbot had used. Our own behavior, I have to admit, was loutish. I hope, when we acknowledged the introductions, we were not surly but we were almost monosyllabic and I'm afraid when we sat down we stared fixedly at Frances.

This had the effect of drawing from her a spate of small talk, delivered in a style that was very close to arch. Previous to reaching with Albert the top rank of playwrights, she had been in the theater and now she was giving a performance of drawing-room comedy of manners that was a pleasure to all of us, though the look behind the smile and in her eyes was giving a message that she hoped each of us would drop dead.

Sophy was the first to rally. It was the Philadelphia strain coming to the surface. She brought sherry to the visitor and engaged him in conversation, relieving Frances momentarily, who seized the moment as a drowning man grasps a life jacket to ask Albert to bring her a vermouth.

Father Talbot, or whatever his appellation, was ample in size and information. He was a true scholar of the church and of Ireland. With the fervor of an evangelist he exhorted us to see Holy Island, proposing hemself as guide. We had planned to go to Holy Island, but not with a guide. We would go tomorrow, he told us, and he would round up two small boats and the boatmen we would require. We were impressed by his scholarliness and touched by his very evident love of the place of Holy Island and its associations, but we were reduced close to abject contrition when, answering my comment about their lovely house on the hill, he said, yes, he and Mrs. Talbot would be sorry to leave it.

"You see," he explained simply, with no trace of self-pity, "the parish must be combined with the one in Killaloe and the property will be sold because, I'm sorry to say, the total number of my parishioners is thirteen."

He was a lonely man hungry for people with whom he could talk, coming down to the quay at the arrival of a new boat he could see from his hilltop, hurrying, hoping he would find, this time, responsive souls who would go with him and learn from him about Holy Island. He struck gold in the *St. Patrick.* We told him this expedition under his guidance would mark the peak of our visit to Ireland.

The expedition was set for the following afternoon and the rector went off with a smiling face and the added cheer of two glasses of sherry inside him.

The scene he left was not a happy one. Frances was the doe at bay, sending off the attackers yapping at her with:

"What else could I do? You can't keep a caller standing on your front porch or whatever that place out there is—of course I had to ask him in."

"You did not have to be specific, saying, 'Come in for a glass of sherry.' That was an invasion of the Shoebag."

She parried this neatly and it was the *coup de grâce.* Smiling sweetly, she answered, "I thought you would mind much more having to wait for your drink."

We allowed Ellen at dinner to tell us something of what we would see since certainly she had been reading about it. She interrupted herself in the middle of the recital.

"I knew there was a connection and I couldn't place it, but now I have it. Talbot and Boswell. You know, Lloyd, the papers." Lloyd's response was not immediate and Ellen was impatient but not clarifying.

"Lloyd, dear," she insisted, "the Castle Malahide."

Like a skin-diver returning to the surface and removing his snorkle, Lloyd, shaking his head, evidently cleared it.

"I've got it," he said, "where the Boswell Papers were found."

"That's exactly what I've been telling you, and the family name is Talbot. Lady Talbot was the one who discovered the papers in an old dungeon in the castle, and correspondence of Sir Joshua Reynolds too, and this rector's name is Talbot. Of course Holy Island has nothing to do with Boswell, but Mr. Talbot's name did make me think of Malahide. Perhaps I'd better go on about Holy Island."

We played the Telephone Game after dinner to Sam's

gratification and triumph in his win over two challenges. Albert was pleased by the rounds of applause that acknowledged the vivid characterizations of the actors and prizefighters on his list.

Alone, by my request, on the boat next morning—even Harvey had been persuaded to go for a walk—I settled down happily to say into my Dictaphone things that had been happening. I was self-conscious when others were within hearing unlike Harvey, who welcomed viewers. After some half-hour of rapid talk from scraps of notes I had jotted on menus, backs of envelopes, whatever was handy, I reversed the lever to catch up on what I had said. The indicator moved all the way across the belt and not a sound came from it. Allowing for moments of despair that the machine had broken down, I realized it needed recharging, a requirement I consistently overlooked. (I am of the third generation of engineers in my family and not one of them has passed down to me a shred of their aptitude for mechanical things.) Pleased with my sharpness of eye and resourcefulness, I remembered an electric outlet in the tub room, the term we used to distinguish it from those that held the Brooklyn, N.Y., johns. Maeve and Anita were doing the cabins when I came down with the machine, explaining my purpose and, modestly, my quick-wittedness in discovering a solution for my dilemma.

"You see," I added, "I bring a transformer"—as though I knew what that was—"when I come abroad."

Maeve asked if she could see it and I handed her the machine and transformer, pleased at her quick interest in anything she had not known before.

"I'm afraid it won't work," she told me, pointing to some lettering I had never noticed on the little gadget. "This takes AC voltage and ours is DC." I knew those letters but not their function.

"You'll get no charge from this outlet, but I've an idea

now. Mr. Logan, I think, might do it for you. He's in the village on the main street directly across from the top of this road. It's a garage that he has but it's a machine shop too, and I've been told he knows a great deal about electricity. I think it may be that he can manage your little machine."

Mr. Logan came from the interior of his shop as I stood in his doorway. He was, I surmised, in his sixties, tall, slim, ruddy-cheeked, with lively brown eyes and a warming friendly smile. As he came toward me, I saw he walked stiffly and was lame. I held out my Dictaphone to him, explaining my need. Instead of taking it from me, he asked me to bring it to a table he indicated. He would not touch it until he had washed his hands because he'd been working on a machine and did not want to get so much as a smudge on mine. He did not allow me to place it on the table until he had put under it a piece of brown wrapping paper. He looked over the instrument carefully and then, carrying it to the window, examined it more thoroughly. He read every word and symbol of printing that was included in the machine proper, and on the extension for charging. After he had finished this inspection he carried it to his own charging apparatus, reread what was printed on mine, examined his own thoroughly. When he gave his opinion I felt a cardiogram, blood tests and X-rays had been taken.

"We can do the charging," he said, "and I am by way of thinking it will come out fine." (An operation was necessary but there would be a full recovery. The patient could return home that night by nine o'clock.) I hurried back to the quay where the Holy Island expedition was to assemble.

Mr. Talbot himself was one of the two boatmen he had engaged to ferry us. Mr. Tierney, to whom we were introduced, ran the other boat and owned them both. Mr. Tierney had brought as his passenger his own dog, Derg, named,

he explained, for the lough. On the way to the island, Derg created distraction and, equally, apprehension. As we pushed off he had jumped into the Talbot boat and, discovering his mistake, was fairly distraught, barking furiously, whimpering, crying, shaking and trying to work his way among the passengers from the bow to the stern. The boat itself was one of two small dories equipped with outboard motors—and responded like me, nervously, to this activity. Halloing to Mr. Tierney to hold back a bit, Mr. Talbot changed his course to edge up alongside the other boat. While there was still a respectable broad-jump distance between them, Derg jumped, landing safely and ecstatically. Mr. Tierney told our boatman he needn't have bothered with this maneuver. Derg would eventually have jumped from the boat and maybe swum to the other but more probably have swum ashore and waited.

"Many a time," said Mr. Tierney, "I've not had the patience to wait for him chasing hares over there and he has swum home from the island." When we had pulled away from the other boat, Mr. Talbot told us more about Tierney. He was over eighty, had been on a full pension but become so bored, he'd gone back to work as a boatman, taking parties to the island and helping boats tie up in the harbor. He was still entitled to full pension but had refused it indignantly and would accept only half.

Thanks to Ellen and my own subsequent reading, I knew a little about Holy Island but there are doubts and differences about its origin and its various functions. Some writers declare positively it was a monastic settlement begun in the seventh century. Another writer says, "It is most probably a Christianized druidic center and its origins therefore lost in that misty dawn of Christianity in the West." Some say it was founded by St. Caimin whose brother was Guaire. Another says the brother was St. Colum. They do agree—

that is, those I have read agree—on a legend of the two brothers. It is to me a lovely crystallization of the charming perversity of the Irish point of view.

The two brothers, according to the legend, were discussing one day what each would do if he were allowed to fill a church with something that would be of the greatest benefit to their fellow men. One of them said he would fill his church all the way to the roof with gold and give it all to the poor. The other brother, derisive of this idea, was asked what his choice would be. His answer was he would fill his church all the way up to the roof with the diseases of the world so that they would be contained there and though the people would have to stay outside, there would be less sickness among them. A preservation of this legend was the belief of miraculous healing powers contained in their church.

Unlike the burial ground at Clonmacnoise, the saints' graveyard on Holy Island, with its stones inscribed in Greek, Celtic and Latin and covering a period from the eighth to the twelfth century, has remained untouched, although down through the centuries the place has been ransacked and attacked time and again. It is believed that the round tower on the island was a place of refuge for the monks, since it was of stone with only one entrance and that high above the ground. The holy men would take their sacred vessels, barricade themselves in the tower and wait there until the pillaging around them was over. Scholars have written about Holy Island. Speculations of origin have been published, but its quality of detachment from the world, its literal unworldliness is not disputable. Clonmacnoise is surrounded by a community and bordered on one side by a highway. Holy Island *is* an island, a place apart and for the single purpose of worship, thirteen centuries of consecrated ground.

Mr. Talbot was knowledgeable and eloquent, interesting to hear and necessary occasionally to get away from and, sitting apart, let the stones and the ground convey their story.

The sunset that night was a benediction. Some of us sat on the stone of the harbor wall until the soft outlines of Tountinna Mountain and the lesser ones below were blended and then lost. We did not play any games that night, choosing instead good talk and early bed.

The next day, Friday, the 13th of October, was for me the golden day of the cruise. The morning was sunny, not flamboyantly because there was a mistiness on the edges and an autumn bite, more of a nibble, in the air. From the top of our road I saw Mr. Logan across the street in front of his garage and machine shop and I waved to him. He called across to me, "Good morning. You'll be coming for your machine, I expect." I was crossing the street. When I reached him he was saying, "I have it here waiting for you. I just came out to smell the air a bit." Taking my hand, he said, smiling, "I haven't got into the grease as yet," and shook it vigorously. What followed, that could have been a commonplace exchange, marked for me indelibly that 13th of October.

"What a lovely day," I said, and this was his answer:

"'Tis that, a lovely *frail* autumn day." All that day I sang to myself and sometimes aloud the word and the phrase "a *frail* autumn day" and please God I will never forget it.

A young woman carrying my machine still on its piece of brown wrapping paper came from the garage. This was his daughter Mary, Mr. Logan told me. She had brown eyes like his, curling black hair. I think she was in her twenties. Like her father, she was friendly, cordial but she had more vivacity than he. She asked if I would come to their house next door and try out the machine there. "I keep it cleaner

189

than my father keeps his place." They grinned at each other.

Following her into the house, I confessed I had stood the day before for some time to admire its exterior. We paused to let me admire again a dramatically beautiful fuchsia tree and at the opposite corner of the front garden the topiary bird, but I told her when I had been looking the day before I had not dreamed I'd have the privilege of actually going into the house, and she blushed a little. We went into a narrow hallway and immediately on the right into the kitchen. It had a flagstoned floor and at the far side from the door a generous open fireplace. Between the door and the fireplace in the center of the room there was a long loaf of fresh-baked bread on a kitchen table. I do not know how I resisted the temptation to steal it, buy it, have it, and I still think about it every once in a while. At Mary's request, when she had put my machine on the table, I inserted the belt I'd brought for testing it, spoke a few words, turned it back to listen, found the charging had worked perfectly. I turned to tell Mary Logan so, and found her watching the operation, eyes sparkling.

"Why," she said, "it talked right back to you, did it not?" After a moment's hesitation she asked diffidently the reason for my using the machine. I explained it was for making notes and observations as I moved about since the instrument was small enough to be carried easily. By talking into it, I could watch at the same time, and this of course was impossible when one had to write it down. After one or two hesitant starts, she asked if I played the notes back to myself when I got home to help me remember the trip. I realized I was as hesitant and embarrassed answering as she had been in the asking, but I said I would play them back many times and hoped they would be the starting point for a book about the trip. Her eyes widened. Her color deepened. "Do you mean a book to take in your hands and read?" Without waiting for my acknowledgment and picking up the machine, she started for the door, calling back to me please to come with her to her father. We found him in his garage and she was talking as we came through the door.

"Father, a book is going to come out of this very machine. The lady talks into it and then by and by she will write down what it says to her and a great deal more and there it will be. Did you ever hear of such a thing?"

"Well, what a thing that is," her father told her, and to me, "When you speak of books to Mary, you are talking of the thing that means the most to her. She's never without a book."

She flashed back instantly, "You're a reader yourself."

He admitted it shamefacedly as if this were something one ought to keep very private. He was equally abashed when I asked the cost for charging my Dictaphone. After considerable thought and with apology lest I find it excessive, he told me twenty pence would be a very full sum. He accepted fifty reluctantly, but very cordially my request—"if it would not be an imposition"—to bring my friends to see their house. Mary was glowing.

"Though," he added, "there's nothing much to see there. It's old but it's plain, and it's clean. Mary is a fine housekeeper, but there are things here and abouts you should certainly be seeing. Have you been to Holy Island?"

He was pleased that we had been, had found it one of the most interesting places visited on the whole cruise and counted ourselves fortunate (fingers a little bit crossed at this) to have had Mr. Talbot as our guide.

"Now then," Mr. Logan said, "that leads to two things. One, a beautiful poem about Holy Island I doubt you've seen."

Mary interrupted, "I have it, Father. I'll be happy to set it down for them."

"She will do that and it will be ready when you come back with your friends. The other place you must surely .

191

visit is the hostel just down the street there. It was originally the residence of Lady Talbot, a very great lady she was, and you see it's all of the same family, but what I hope you will notice in particular is the oak tree that's there, and you are fortunate to be coming this way when you did because that great tree is going to have to be cut down and it's a sadness for all of us. Experts have come from far and wide to see it and tell us it's two thousand years old and the second largest in the whole of the British Isles. But these experts have said it will go down in the next heavy storm with terrible damage and if it should fall across the road and people and cars passing by, there would be killings surely."

Clearly the tree itself was dear to Mr. Logan and the matter of its destruction a subject of wide interest and concern. It required no imagination to picture the discussions and the arguments and the eloquence in the pubs.

"The difficulty," he was saying, "is with the cutting down. No one as yet will undertake the labor. There are sixty tons of lumber in that single tree."

By what arguments and bets laid, I wondered, had that figure been reached and agreed to? There had been pride in Mr. Logan's voice when he began, but as he ended there was only sadness. He almost shook himself visibly and changed the subject. When would my friends like to see his house? I told him I would find them as quickly as possible because there was not much time. We had been told at breakfast we would leave at quarter past eleven. I went down the hill as fast as I could manage with the machine in its case hanging by a strap from my shoulder and whacking me behind the knee. Thankfully I left it at the boat on the first chair inside the lounge. There was no one in sight but I called down the stairs in the hope there might be some stragglers, and voices answered.

"Come out, come out, whoever you are," I called back urgently. "I've got something to show you." Ellen, Sophy,

Mildred and Sam came quickly up the stairs. They had started off together for a walk but the day had been so warm, they'd come back to change coats for light sweaters. They were delighted by the invitation to see Mr. Logan's house. As we started off, the General suggested perhaps she'd better check with Maeve the time we were to leave. She would catch up with us. When she did, she was breathless because she had been running. She had found Maeve in the galley and Maeve had said quarter past eleven surely.

Mr. Logan and Mary were waiting for us outside their house. We stopped as I had stopped to admire the fuchsia and the topiary figure. He was shyly pleased at our praise, admitting he did it himself; it was a hobby. I do not know how he managed it and obviously I could not ask. Including the base on which it stood, the figure was certainly ten feet tall and Mr. Logan was crippled with arthritis. He was chuckling as he told us he was the topiary artist. Not a week before, he said, he had seen and overheard a couple standing in front of the figure. He learned later they'd come from Dublin. He had heard the girl say, "Look at that beautiful figure of a horse," and her boy companion saying, "What a fool you are. Did you ever see a horse with two legs?"

Mr. Logan laughed, wiping his eyes and inviting us to share the humor. "Do you not think that one of the most ridiculous things? I meant it for a peacock and I'm admitting the tail is too short but I gave it only two legs and I'd never do that for a horse." And he repeated, "Is that not ridiculous?" We agreed, joyously because his own enjoyment was so infectious.

"It's made of whitethorn, you know." He was serious again. "The blackthorn is what we use for walking sticks in Ireland. The whitethorn is used for the topiaries. In spring it's all in bloom and white, and a lovely sight it is."

They stopped again as I had stopped outside the house to

193

exclaim over the ivy. It was unfamiliar even to Ellen, though she knew it was an English species. Mr. Logan agreed, adding it was very old and very useful because it kept the house dry. Ellen accepted this doubtfully because she said she would have thought it would work into the stones and separate them. Mr. Logan denied this.

"It's the very opposite," he said. "It holds them together and that's particularly how it keeps them dry."

When we went into the kitchen I saw what I had not noticed on my first visit. I can only suppose it was because I had been so distracted by the sight and smell of the fresh-baked loaf of bread. In the center of the open fireplace was a stove fitted with a pipe that went up behind it through the roof. When Sam asked what they burned in it, Mary took from a box by the side of the stove a square of perhaps eight inches and held it out to him. Sam was delighted.

"Peat," he said. "It's the first I've seen. Now I know what Irish peat is."

Mary smiled. "Well, sir, that's what they call it in England, and we're the people who use it, but it's not what we call it at all. In Ireland we call it turf."

Simultaneously we exclaimed our incredulity, talking over one another. "But you always hear of Irish peat and read about the peat bogs in Ireland. You don't associate peat with England at all."

Mary was indulgent. "Well anyway that's how it is. With us it's turf." She saddened, shaking her head. "But I'm not sure we can continue to use it. My father has arthritis and he probably cannot go up another winter to cut it." She wrinkled her nose. "So we'll have to change and make it that diesel oil."

Mildred asked where their turf came from and Mary, pointing vaguely in the distance, said, "Oh, off up there, in the banks."

To Sophy's question of who owned it, she answered, "Oh, it always goes with the house." While she was talking I had moved over to the end of the room that looked on the street and sat on a broad sill so low I had a full view of the outdoors.

When they had stopped talking about the turf, I asked her about the three or four very heavy hooks I had noticed from where I sat and had wondered about. They were embedded in the ceiling, and I could not imagine their purpose. My friends noticed them for the first time and were equally mystified. Mary was pleased by our interest; in her new experience, I think, of being teacher and guide she had lost her earlier embarrassment and was talking eagerly. The hooks, she told us, were for hanging pork in the old days and she described the process. The pigs were killed outside, of course, and, heavily salted, put in barrels for some six weeks or so. Then they were brought in and hung on those hooks.

"You had to be very nimble going to and fro because the salt dripped, but by and by it hardened, and when this was done, you would take down a side and slice from it what you wanted of bacon. Then there were always special picees put aside. We called those pork steaks. But people don't do that any more, so a great many have removed the hooks and it was an enormous task because they were embedded deep in the rafters, and now they're regretting they ever took them down, it was such a terrible job. But my father certainly didn't leave them there because of that. He says they remind him of the old days and he likes that and so do I."

We were not invited to see any of the other rooms in the house, only because, I think, she perceptively felt this the most interesting to us, but she did ask if we would like to step to the back. "The back" was a charming cobblestoned courtyard or patio with an arbor at one end, vine-covered, and beyond that a building also vine-covered, probably a

barn, but making a natural boundary for this outdoor room.
I was not surprised to hear Sam behind me say to Mildred:
"Now this is it. This is really it. I'll be very tactful about
asking Mr. Logan if he'd sell it, but he's got bad arthritis
and Mary's worried about him, and that girl is too intelligent
to be cut off here in the village, and we'll certainly keep
those hooks in the ceiling and disturb as little as possible,
and the barn, if that's what it is, will be a guesthouse. I tell
you, Mildred, it will be wonderful, living here and talking
to the people—"

Ellen had overheard too and was visibly alarmed.

"Oh, Sam, I'm sure that ivy doesn't really keep out the
damp. You know Mr. Logan has got arthritis and they say
peat or turf is very hard to cut properly."

Mildred smiled at Ellen. "Not to worry, dear," she said,
and slipping her arm through his, "Come on, Sam."

Mary had copied the poem about Holy Island and slipped
it to me as we were leaving. I said we would like to tell her
father goodbye and she ran ahead of us to fetch him from the
garage.

Mr. Logan said he was pleased we liked the house, "though
'tis a simple one, but it's done for those that came before me
and one day it will be for Mary to do with as she pleases."

Sam caught him up. "Well, Mr. Logan, perhaps—" Mildred shook her head. "Sam . . ." she said. "Perhaps you don't
have many visitors," she ended rather lamely.

Mary spoke to me quickly, as if she'd been gathering her
courage to do it.

"Knowing from your speech you are Americans, would it
be possible you come from New York? Can you do your
writing there? It's a very, we call it 'bigga' place, so I've been
told."

I told her I did live there, that it was a "bigga" place but
that I managed to do my writing in a very small corner of

it, and we both laughed. Mr. and Mrs. Garrison, I said, came from New York, too; Mr. and Mrs. Jaffe had lived many years in California but now lived in London, and the others in our group, Mr. and Mrs. Hackett, lived in New York and wrote plays there but Mr. and Mrs. Stevenson lived in Connecticut.

"It may not be worth mentioning," Sophy contributed, "but I live in New York, too. In fact," indicating me, "we are neighbors, and that is a little unusual because in a big city it's more likely your neighbors are not your friends and vice versa."

"Now this is a friendly place," Mr. Logan told us. "Everyone speaks to everyone else whether he's a stranger to you or not. We say here you must be particularly careful about speaking to a stranger—"

"Well, that's true in New York," Ellen said half to herself.

"—because," Mr. Logan continued, "maybe he's standing up there on the corner looking about which way to turn and if he's Irish and you don't speak to him, he will be very offended and likely to start some trouble, because he'll think that you are considering yourself better than him."

"And *that* is certainly Irish," I murmured to Sophy.

Mr. Logan heard me and was pleased. "'Tis that," he concurred. He had been looking away, but he turned back to us smiling.

"Round about them orchards sweep,
Apple and peach tree fruited deep . . .

On that pleasant morn of the early fall,"

he said.

The words sounded familiar and their familiarity brought to me a curious uneasiness, an association with some other place and circumstance.

198

"Surely you must know that poem. It's by your own poet, John Greenleaf Whittier."

"Barbara Frietchie," we told him as one voice.

"We heard it recited only a few days ago," I added, "by one of your countrymen." I knew very well now the association and the reasons for my uneasiness.

Mr. Logan added, "Every schoolboy in Ireland has learned that poem and can recite it by heart from beginning to end."

"Isn't that wonderful!" Again we were a chorus—a loud one. "I wish we had time to hear you say it all. I'm afraid we must go now."

Recognizing the signs of departure as we shook hands all around and thanked him again, Mr. Logan urged us not to go back without seeing Lady Talbot's house. It was down the road only a bit and on the opposite side. Pointing, he said it was less than a hundred yards.

We found it, of course, without difficulty, recognizing from the gates and inner courtyard this was a place of consequence. As we were looking through the tall handsome gates and trying to see beyond the courtyard, a man came into view from our left. He was short and stocky, with red hair and blunt features. His companions were one of the most beautiful Pekinese I have ever seen and a top-quality Springer spaniel. He invited us eagerly to come in and let him show us the place, asking us at the same time to wait a bit while he closed in the dogs. When he had opened the gates he led us immediately to the place from which he had come, a charming little house behind a fenced-in garden where the two dogs were begging for attention.

"Give them a pat, do," he urged. "They're wanting to welcome you, and that fellow there," pointing to the Pekinese, "is the most welcoming of the two of them, but he's a wicked fellow certainly. He can win ribbons and cups over

199

any dog in the whole of Ireland and Great Britain too, but let a judge stoop down to look him over, he'll be bitten for his pains. He knows more than most human beings." Somewhat ambiguous, I thought, but Irish "certainly."

Our host, whose name we never learned, told us the cottage was his. It had been the caretaker's lodge and he had been the caretaker—steward, he called it. He led us across the courtyard and a little beyond it where we had the first view of a magnificent house on a hilltop, the lawns and gardens stretching behind it to a superb view of the water and the hills and mountains beyond.

Lady Talbot had come every year even after her husband had died until she felt too old to make the journey. "But," he said, "they never sell anything in that family, that they don't." So she had given the place to be used as a youth hostel. "If you'd care to see the visitors' book, you'd find there names of young people from India to Iceland."

These visitors were given cooking facilities and lodging. They brought sleeping bags but very few of them had blankets and so blankets were kept on hand to distribute. He showed us where the stables had been and the coach houses and I noticed an area of overgrown grass that had obviously been a tennis court. We could not go in because the season was over and the matron was not there, but we looked through the windows. At the sight of beautiful high-ceilinged rooms with exquisite paneling and delicate chandeliers I could not help feeling a pang that, marvelous as it was for those young people, great style and the grand manner had gone. Ellen asked if this were not the family in whose place the great Boswell Papers had been found and our guide fairly capered with pleasure.

"Now you've got it exactly," he said, beaming at Ellen. "It was not only at their own place, Malahide, those papers were discovered but 'twas Her Ladyship herself that was the discoverer. Down in the dungeon they were or maybe it was up in the attic, but one or the other it was and what she was doing in either of them places I've never been told, but 'twas her found the treasure and the great treasure it was, they say."

We assured him it was one of the great treasures for all time and he thanked us for our appreciation.

"Now," he said, "I would like to show you another great treasure, and 'tis your good fortune that you've come here this very day because the next time you're passing by you'll not find it here."

He was leading the way beyond the onetime stables and when he stopped he had no need to point out nor identify the treasure. It was the most magnificent oak tree any of us, we agreed, had ever seen. We said we had heard about it from Mr. Logan and how badly he felt. The steward unabashedly rubbed a hand across his eyes.

"I don't want to hear those woodchoppers at work." he said huskily. "When that day comes, I'm going to take my dogs and stay in the back country somewhere till it's all over, and I'm not going to tell Her Ladyship a word about it, and that will be the only time I've not reported every single thing to her. And she likes to know too, every bit about the place—and the dogs, though they're mine too, a gift from her along with my house and a little land."

It was impossible to miss the sight of Biffy and Lloyd as we came down the hill. They were standing on the quay alongside the boat, each with arm extended to emphasize a concentrated scrutiny of his wristwatch, and each tapping a foot so spectacularly it could almost have been a one-legged step dance. We knew the reason for this performance. At each time of departure, they had been the stragglers, following the call or flash of a bird just a little farther on. This was their hour, at least minute, of triumph, to be the first

201

ones back and they were savoring it fully. According to Sophy, we were five minutes late. Frances and Albert were even later, but only by a few minutes. They had taken a longer way home and come round the road to the quay from the direction opposite to ours. The General reported to Maeve that everyone was aboard and she could tell Anthony. Maeve assured her it was indeed a very "foine" thing we were back so promptly but the only thing about our taking off was that Anthony was not aboard.

"You see," she said, "he has so many friends all up and down the river and they all come together in the pub certainly."

Anita was sent up the hill to find him and came back twenty minutes later cheerful about the message she brought

that Anthony had been on his way to the boat surely, but on his way, with no thought on his mind but leaving, he had run into a man so surprised at the sight of him, thinking not to see him again this summer, he had forced a return to the pub and another jar. "He'll be along very soon now, but he could not end the season with an insult to a friend certainly. I tell you, confident-like," she added, "he is a remarkable man for friends."

The remarkable man reached the boat at half past twelve. He swung aboard with a cheery wave to all of us on deck.

"I hope we're not badly off schedule," I could not resist saying. I did not need to hear his reply. Any one of us could have given it, but he said it just the same, calling down from his captain's perch above,

"Time enough. Time enough."

During lunch we exchanged incidents of the morning. Albert and Frances had had, in their opinion and, when we heard it, ours, an interesting conversation with a man. On their roundabout way home after buying postcards in the village, they had seen two rather small houses very close to each other and identical in pattern. In front of these a man was raking soil, obviously preparing to sow grass seed. Seeing them looking from one to the other of the houses he had dropped his rake and come over to say it was a lovely day and were they interested in the houses. They had said they were not interested in purchasing the one that was obviously empty. Albert interposed:

"Frances was apologetic about this, afraid of hurting the man's feelings." He had been breathless, as he put it, with apprehension she was going to enter into negotiation and they would find themselves in New York, absentee landlords of a house in Mount Shannon, Ireland. He had averted this crisis "and I was sweating by the time I got Madam distracted from her obligation to buy," asking the man what his involvement was, a godsend of distraction because the man was eager to tell. He and a friend were the builders of the two houses. They had owned the property but had had no previous experience in building. They had made some mistakes and run into some trouble getting them straightened out. When the house was finished they had not felt like trying out another pattern, so they had built the second exactly like the first, and made no mistakes at all. One of the houses had been sold and was occupied, the other was very close to a sale. Albert had breathed a little more easily hearing that. The occupants were Germans. There was quite a German colony round about, the builder had told them, and more were coming every year. This owner was a doctor and his wife a dentist. They had children and they came three times a year. They had boats too and loved the water. "Money is not scarce with them either." The doctor had made it known his grandfather was Irish and the wife's grandmother was too. That was the reason they had come to Ireland. Harvey asked rhetorically why, did we think, they thought it necessary to make known their Irish background. Lloyd commented ruminatively he was inclined to doubt its veracity and thought it an invention in order to ingratiate themselves in the community. Opinions flashed back and forth among the tables and as I joined in I thought how curious it was we should all become so involved in two houses most of us had never seen and probably never would see, nor the occupants of one, but there was the making of a mystery story, almost my favorite kind of literature, if one had the special ability I envied, to develop it. Mildred asked if the Hacketts had seen the inside of the houses and Frances told her the builder had taken them into the one that was unfurnished and they had looked through the windows of the other.

"Very commonplace," Frances told her. "Square rooms,

204

department-store furniture, the latest gadgets in the kitchen, but the view from the back was glorious, down a steep hill, almost a cliff, but with bushes and trees and then out across the water. But it would be very disagreeable to live so close to your neighbor."

"So you see, Sam," Mildred told him, "it really wouldn't do."

Sam betrayed his thoughts by a startled look and a slight pause. "Unless," he said, "we took the other one for the children. Did you ask the price?"

Albert had asked. "He hoped to get twenty-five thousand for the one not yet sold and it would be finished by next March."

"From what you've told me I'd say this was an Irish exaggeration."

"Leave it alone, Sam," was Mildred's suggestion, and changed the subject.

The sound of Maeve's heels briskly tapping along the gangway outside the windows was as effective as a captain's orders to leave the tables and come outside. We were in time to watch our approach to the tiny harbor of Garry-kennedy, at its land end the lonely splintered remnant of the old Norman watchtower that was one of the first things Harvey had sketched at the very beginning of our cruise. I heard Sophy tell Sam now we were in Lough Derg again but Sam was preoccupied, watching Maeve's every move with the rope and making abortive gestures of assistance. At the moment she was about to cast the rope, a small motor cruiser slipped past us and into the passage ahead too narrow for accommodating us both. From the bridge Anthony waved and called and, when he had got their attention, made with gestures a request to let us come in ahead since ours was so much the larger boat. I overheard two of our sailors, Sophy and Lloyd, agreeing on the reason for this request.

"Anthony's got to tie up bow and stern because there's quite a wind blowing up. Our stern will be outside if they tie in ahead, but if they tie up to us, they'll still be in the slip and protected if we get a blow."

"Don't let Sam hear you," I asked them. "I doubt that Mildred's brought lemon drops."

Obligingly the smaller boat backed from the slip and as it passed we recognized its occupants and waved to them. We had seen them moored along the quay at Mount Shannon. Mildred and I had noticed them particularly because coming upstairs at the same time that morning we had seen through the door the men of our party on the deck in silent concentration on something beyond, and coming up behind them had discovered, with nudges of enjoyment to each other, the object of their rapt attention, a girl sitting on the stone wall of the quay combing her long yellow hair. I had said "Boo" and Harvey had very nearly fallen overboard. The other occupants of the boat we saw now were a slim young boy and an older couple, the woman with very short bushy hair, the man heavy-set with a beard. As soon as we had moored, they came in again behind us and tied up to the stern of our boat. We went back as soon as we had come ashore to thank them for their courtesy in yielding their first place. They were Dutch, they told us, here on a "big holiday," and that was almost the extent of their English.

As we walked along the road to the tiny village I knew why our return to Banagher when we met the Jaffes had been of such happy moment to us. It was because Garrykennedy, our first stop, was a village of neglect. There was the junk-yard I remembered, full of derelict cars and other scraps, a few small scattered houses with a pub between almost every two of them, no gardens in front, only weeds and broken-down baby carriages or other junk around the doorways. Banagher had been our introduction to the Ireland we'd come to see.

Our walk was short but during our time away a caller had arrived, the only one on our cruise other than Mr. Talbot. This was an oversized wirehaired black-and-white spotted terrier of sorts. She was lying in our doorway from the deck watching with friendly interest our approach. Maeve too was glad to see us, she said. Anthony was a little impatient to be under way again, in case there should be a blow that would hold up our getting back to Mount Shannon at the scheduled time to meet Ruth Field. I knew this had been an excursion planned to give a variety of scene during the hours before her arrival, but I would not have chosen Garrykennedy as its terminal. I had a feeling strong enough to be a conviction the selection had been Anthony's, and a contributing factor to it the availability and number of pubs. The more pubs the more friends he would find. Finding Anthony was not difficult but it took time. After Anita had gone up the road to fetch him we decided, in view of the number of establishments to visit, a larger search party was required. Therefore the full strength of the company left the boat again, this time with an added member, our visiting dog. Like us she had a purpose. Leading the way, she stopped at the door of each of the pubs waiting to have it opened. Before we found Anthony she had reached her goal and come trotting out with it: another dog much like her in ambiguity of breed but smaller. It was quite obvious she had wanted her friend to have a glimpse of the strangers.

Anita found Anthony in a pub we had overlooked; she knew them all. We turned back to the boat, the dogs following us all the way to the quay; then in their own fashion saying goodbye by sniffing our heels, they turned round and returned to the village.

Anthony told us he'd been detained because the Dutch people had asked him to untie their boat for them and of course we could not get away until they had left. I was endeavoring to visualize the sleight of hand required to untie from a pub the boat attached to ours but Anthony, perhaps feeling we were slow of comprehension, explained further. He had been a bystander while the young Dutch boy engaged in a heavy transaction with the publican that involved swapping some very large pocket knives, evidently brought from Holland, for whatever the publican had to offer of equal value. The rest of the party had of course been unable to leave without the boy, so it would have been futile for Anthony to come back ahead of them.

"And surely," Anthony concluded, "there's"—we could have finished it for him—"time enough." Since Anthony never showed the slightest effect of whatever number of jars friends and good manners had forced upon him and since we always did reach our destination with "time enough," we could not chide him and we tried not to fume. Sophy and I having had experience in each country could only say to each other that, like the Greeks, the Irish showed, in their way, an indifference to time.

The Dutch group returned, Anthony helped them get under way and back on the bridge again signaled Maeve to cast off. Sam was at her side. As she stooped to bring back on board our little gangplank, he waved her off, telling her he would take care of that. He did and in the process swept from the deck a doormat always placed there to take care of muddy shoes after a walk. Mortified, Sam, peering out into the water where it floated, muttered, "Sorry about that. Have to have a retake."

This is the poem Mary wrote down for us:

Where the Shannon's rolling flood onward sweeps unto the
sea,
Lies a little wavewashed island emerald green and fair to
see,
With its lofty watchtower pointing like a finger in the sky,
And its gabled ruins standing tell of fame in days gone by.
'Neath its shadow in the graveyard lie the holy men at rest,
And on each rough stone that marks them strangely traced
their names on earth.
These the men who from the tower top saw the dreaded
Danes sail by
To raid their island, drown its treasures in Loug Derg's
blue waters nigh.
Down the centuries toiling, teaching, going forth to lands
afar,
Of the gospel story preaching silenced not by prison bar.
Then a cruel king gave his decree: "Get you hence! no
more return,
Nought shall be upon this island save what fires refuse to
burn."
Slowly, sadly, when departing knelt one of them on the shore
To pray forgiveness be granted unto them that evil bore.
And lo, where he had knelt to pray a little spring appeared,
Its waters laughed to meet the day and down the slope
careered.
And onward still it flows unto this day,
And those who kneel beside a prayer may say,
But of its waters taste not 'til they grasp
Their foeman's hand again in friendship's clasp.

—Anon.

From Marion J. Logan
Ivy House,
Mountshannon
Co. Clare,
Ireland

Harvey Stevenson's watercolor of the Norman watchtower at Garrykennedy

# The Finale

Ruth's arrival carried the same quality of unreality the Jaffes' had brought. When you have been in a world detached from accustomed measures of distance, places and time, it is difficult to adjust your sights and your other senses. We had been cruising for twelve days, and had reached in that time a spot distant from Shannon Airport by an hour and a half in a car. We had seen only simple conveyances and clothes like the ones we were wearing. A limousine, a very smartly dressed woman alighting from it, made us blink, but only for a moment. The rush of feet that followed, the cries of welcome, the joyous embraces, like a closing accordion, squeezed out all distances between us. There was no need of introductions except to Maeve and Anita. We scarcely gave her time to change her shoes before we hurried her up the hill to a quick view of the charming village, and brought her back for tea and Maeve's fresh hot cakes.

Like the Jaffes, Ruth was surprised and pleased by the size of the *St. Patrick* and its accommodations. Considering, we told her, she must have had an impression of our sleeping in tiered bunks, we thought it brave of her to join the party, but wondered if perhaps this had been an underlying reason for her allowing us only two days between stays in Paris and London. She denied this vehemently, insisting it had all been a matter of timing. In her schedule there hadn't been time enough for more than this. Understandably she was bewildered by our outburst of rude laughter when we heard that phrase. "Explanations later," we told her. "Or you may discover it for yourself."

Tea was interrupted for a few minutes when we cast off; we wanted Ruth to see Maeve's efficiency and her high heels and, because Ruth is an experienced and enthusiastic sailor, to enjoy Able Seaman Sam and his nautical language. She was impressed by both. All of us came on deck again after tea. The late-afternoon air was chilly but the sunset Ruth pronounced judicially "reason enough in itself for coming." We tied up in Killaloe only a few yards beyond our point of departure and this time I was aware we all watched the process, not to show it to the newcomer, but because of the realization we would not see it again.

The Telephone Game that night might have been dispirited; we were all unhappily aware this was our last night together. Thanks to reprehensible deals between Ruth and Sam, coached and backed by Mildred, swapping politicians and poets for motion-picture producers and modern painters, the game was at times acrimonious, consistently noisy and continued by proposals and arguments shouted from stateroom to stateroom after we had gone to bed.

Next day we drove in a bus to Galway, poked about the market in the square, stopped to wonder and flinch at a small urchin seven or eight years old, singing with total recall and in a shrill nasal voice one song after another, not one of them with less than four verses. He was doing this for charity, a sign alongside him read. As each of us dropped

213

a contribution into the receptacle indicated, hoping this might be reason for an intermission, the singer nodded, permitting himself no other interruption. We lunched on plaice at the Imperial Hotel that was no different from the average city hotel. We walked up and down the main street briefly, looking halfheartedly into shopwindows. Our hearts were not in Galway. Our hearts were on the *St. Patrick* and heavy in the knowledge we were leaving it. We were on our way back by early afternoon, happy to see country landscape again. Each of the four or five times Sam pointed out to Mildred a farm that might be for sale she would pat Ellen's arm reassuringly.

We stopped in Killaloe at a center we had been told about, for local crafts. It was called Crowe's Shop, and measured up to everything we had been told. Those of us who came back with packages of lovely materials, from tweeds to soft challis, sweaters, ties, discovered others more intelligent than we had left their purchases at the shop to be sent direct to America. This led to a slight tension in the air between the know-it-alls and dull-witted, with exchanges of "Why didn't you tell us?" and "All you had to do was ask." Thanks to the Shoebag Hour, the tension melted almost at its birth.

There was no Telephone Game. We sat talking of do-you-remember-this? and will-you-ever-forget? until we could not delay longer going below to put into bags what we had brought, and endeavor to apply enough pressure to force the acceptance of the extras we had accumulated.

The Jaffes and the Hacketts left at eight o'clock in the morning for Shannon Airport, the Garrisons at ten by car for more sightseeing and visits to friends. The Stevensons went after an early lunch for a later plane from Shannon. When all the rest had gone we took off again, Ruth, Sophy, and I, for a beautiful never-to-be-forgotten four hours' cruise. It was a frail day.

214

The train we were to take to Dublin left Bird Hill Station at eight fifteen next morning. We had breakfasted and were ready at a quarter past seven, the time emphatically stipulated, but Mr. Kearsley, who was to drive us to the station, had not yet arrived. When he came some thirty minutes later, he was blissfully unaware of the gap. Maeve and Anita had struggled up the steep flight of stairs from the landing carrying with our help all our bags, coats and packages that had not been accommodated in the luggage, and the luggage could not be accommodated in the "boot" of the little car. We accommodated the overflow in our laps and around our feet. Mercifully for me, this cut off our view, because what followed was the most hair-raising ride I have ever experienced and as the dear Irish people we were leaving behind would have said, "Praise be to God" I have not had the like since, and "Praise be to God" I could not see the other cars we passed, the hedges we clipped and the corners we cut.

The train was in the station when we arrived. Halloing loudly, Mr. Kearsley drew up beside a narrow arched opening in a tall hedge. This was the only passageway between the car park and the station platform. Answering his call, the conductor, the baggage man, the stationmaster and an innocent bystander, recruited as the officials flashed by, converged in the passageway, got wedged, backed and charged again in single file. Like football players they clasped each piece of baggage, coat or whatever, as Mr. Kearsley and his passengers hurled them. They ran and so did we down the platform toward the end of the train. The forward end seemed to be mail and baggage cars, not that I paused to make sure. The conductor was the first up the steps of the coach. Bags were tossed to him, and from my sensation when mounting, I think I was too. Ruth, Sophy and I, breathing heavily, staggered into the nearest seats. They happened to have been turned to face each other. We had not breath nor vitality enough for taking off our coats, but simultaneously we leaned toward the windows for a last look. The train was in motion. It passed Mr. Kearsley talking to the stationmaster. They waved. It passed the arched opening where the scrimmage had taken place. It was empty now, except for Sophy's largest bag, squarely in the center of it. There had not been quite time enough.

74 75 76 77 10 9 8 7 6 5 4 3 2 1

K3

ATLANTIC OCEAN

NORTHERN IRELAND

LOUGH KEYS
CARRICK-ON-SHANNON
R. Boyle
R. Shannon

LANESBOROUGH

LOUGH REE
ATHLONE
CLONMACNOISE
Galway
CLONFERT
Shannon Harbour
PORTUMNA
BANAGHER
Birr Castle
Dublin

Mountshannon
LOUGH DERG
Holy Is.
Dromineer
KILLALOE
Garrykennedy
Shannon Airport
Ballina
Limerick

IRE L

ATLANTIC OCEAN

ATLANTIC OCEAN

IRISH SEA

St. George's Channel